CW01481109

THE TRANSIENT GUEST

Po Wah Lam

MINERVA PRESS
MONTREUX LONDON WASHINGTON

THE TRANSIENT GUEST
Copyright © Po Wah Lam 1995

All Rights Reserved

No part of this book may be reproduced in any form,
by photocopying or by any electronic or mechanical means,
including information storage or retrieval systems,
without permission in writing from both the copyright owner
and the publisher of this book.

ISBN 1 85863 621 3

First Published 1995 by
MINERVA PRESS
1 Cromwell Place
London SW7 2JE

Printed in Great Britain by
B.W.D. Ltd., Northolt, Middlesex.

THE TRANSIENT GUEST

For a very particular village

"...in concerning the Xinjiang rumour of May 31st. It has now been officially announced by the Party Central Committee that no such thermonuclear activities nor explosions had ever taken place during that date nor near the region as previously reported...."

Excerpt from the
"South China Morning Post"
31st August 1989, Hong Kong

CONTENTS

THE ANCESTRAL HALL

HE SAT STILL like a pointless block of wood. Groaning now and again and enveloped by the echo of a cuckoo. Watching the sand wasp, the walls crumbling. Sometimes around the entrance of holiness and a chorale of wind, he found it a necessity to forget. He looked up to the flare of light indecisively combing through the clouds. The smell of the air, earth and creatures. He knew a storm was coming.

There was a kind of Ancestral Hall, (for worship) village based; they called it ChooTong. He sat there, old, lonely and unwanted. Stray cats were churning before him. They were ginger and white, one-eyed and sometimes adrifts of black. His solid body wedged against the lintel of granite. His dusty pith hat, his cats. Always counting them. Seven, eight, nine. Nine. There were ten, eleven, before that. An elderly man who appears tattered and charred who counts near evening the remaining cat numbers before the clasp of tumbling night. His huge proletariat hands clasping an empty cup. He groans again. Looking up, through the nothingness, he knows someone will come. Someone.

Near the fall of light she brings him a refill of tea. Then the filling for his stomach. She hands him the bones and rice, and he, in turn, dislodges it into this rusty dish, banging it. She loves the way he does this, she has been waiting for this, the way those dabs of black and white and ginger and ripples of fur drift madly toward him, which are like divided continents upon a map. Butterfly patches. One cat, she can see, has only one dark spot within a sea of white. So as it moves it was more like the shadow of a graceful cloud. She names this one Pirate, because its other eye is mysteriously missing.

Have you eaten? he would always ask. She places together her bony knees and sits beside him. He sips tea from a chipped cup normally used in holy ceremonies. Suddenly there is a ricochet in the background, its echo lasting a few milliseconds. She twitches. She looks behind herself as she always does into the dim interior. Holiness. A table and some tablet of words. A standing structure where she felt safe and felt friendship, where the gods were also living. This renovation of harmony.

He has stopped eating now. He too looks behind himself. Giggles. I am going to end here, he says. *They* will come for me here. You had better go now. It's late, not safe. She nods. He has told her this many times before.

A rhapsodic breeze, lapping his coastal memory. There are yarns told around an old man's life among the child of silence. She comes like an absconded feather. A girl who found him nearly bleeding to death near the old school. An elderly man who has no papers nor identity, but is now cared for by her like a pet.

She could hear his stories. But she never speaks. A Mute. Feeding lost creatures others have left behind. In a holy space, forgotten, but has stood well as crowds of masonry savagely crumble with the passing of each rain.

She comes to the dead place looking for life. An area loosely fortified, a collected community within walls. Silence now. A possible explosion. A man uninvited. She brings whatever scraps of food she can find. Affection from things, whether religion or the old man or the swirl of cats. She comes looking for love.

Such a long time, he told her. He had stopped counting the days he had left the lands from beyond, the Tang Frontier as he calls it, the Middle Kingdom.

At the fall of light a trickle of his past may also fall. When not watching that sand wasp descending the cracked wall, or the jagged poise of ceramic tiles ready to fall before him. Remembering dreams. The howling graveyards. The abstention from sleep.

The girl takes the empty rice bowl from his hands. But his hands do not move – they have kept the shape of the bowl. Staring into them as if at a book or a mirror. Just staring.

For such a long time he dreams the same dream. Darkness. There is only the vermin squeak of the rolling rails as he is lowered further and further, sometimes slower, sometimes dangerously fast and out of control. Always feeling he has reached the earth's core –

but he does not stop. Somewhere above him, there is a distant mock of macaws – the jungle. But he is far from heaven, far from life.

He is supine, feeling less a physical being than the day before. Feeling he is always going down. Feelings in a dream. The squeak. The darkness. Himself.

Then, suddenly, he realises he is being lowered down into a tomb.

The girl is always watching the slip slide of tabbies when he is talking. It is television to her. She wants to touch them but can't. They seem to fear her, suddenly vanishing like a wish of flight. Except he, always there for her, waiting, sitting and mumbling in a bucolic habit. His hat as if welded to his skull. This gives him character and recognition which she loves most. She reaches towards the rim, wanting to try it for size but he stops her. No, can't take it off. Ugly! Where I was burnt. Should have died really. Like Palladius...

He starts to giggle, flatly sipping his tea.

There was gas, you see. Palladius struck gas – trapped there millions of years beneath the bed of the tomb. Could have been crossbows, collapsible passages or smeared poison. But ay, what a surprise ... it was brilliant! Nothing like it in all my years! And Palladius, he was down there with a smoke in his mouth. Not even felt the explosion. My head on fire – my back. Cannot smother it, had to hold on. I was pulled up by my capturer. Dogs! It was a mistake. They could not have known who we were. Palladius could not have known he was dead. I felt the fire of his ghostly aftermath.

Do not go that way! He is always warning her of dangers, walls and entrances which hang on air like nervous booby traps. Beside the frequent wander of a huge boar there are also trespassers. Illegal, just like him, but devious. Hands that may scoop her away in darkness and sell her like fowl once cross the thresholds of South China. Vehicles, televisions, thieves and murderers disappear beyond that way. Beyond law. So he warns her again.

Shadows coming behind in the jungle. It was not a language of his own. Huge stone faces and then dark faces surrounding him. Who are you? What happened down there? *Talk!* – if you want to live! Dead bodies and smoke littered his darkness. There was only him now. He was the only member left alive, nearly alive. In the slur of the unconscious. The men all dead, Palladius was dead, the villagers were gone, all so suddenly as he emerged from darkness and light and into the lap of such phantom executioners. They must be either bandits or rogues. Nobody would dare attack the Peoples Army. There must be some bad mistake. Someone kicking or butting him with the ends of an AK rifle as he lay there useless. Macai-h? Aramasdi? Bu-dong... He muttered to them in every language he knew, hoping they would let him alone, to sleep and die, not knowing how badly he was burned. Being dragged through the jungle was all he could remember. Hanging onto a flaming rope. His flaking hands.

He remembers seeing the rope just ahead of him.

Suddenly, in the tomb there was no sound. The chiselling stopped. Palladius had stopped work. A pause, a ticklish suck of air. He ignores it. More flutters of dust. He walks again. Turns – only to be embalmed in flames.

Suddenly his world being filled with light.

Whips of dust riding in a doorway, like ghostly sea horses. He recalls nothing, a feeling that is good. The girl sometimes could be sitting with him anywhere, near darkness, at the parapet or under the shade of a tower. Her silent tug of his thick arm, feeling the throttling vibration of his voice she so much loved. He keeps describing to her his earlier life, how archaeology was more a necessity of survival and not of choice. 1967. 1968. Years of sacrilege. In a time before you were born.

We were not grave robbers. It was all official. But that time was different. In another land, another culture. Someone else's law. Night and day the great stone faces of Angkor kings stood forever around us. So were the terrible birds and sweat and the PLA soldiers. But the scientific value was worth it. No. This was not in China. You will not know it. Far away, amoy. Far, far away.

If now I start closing my eyes I see *them*. If not being dragged through the jungle – I am on fire. Being chased by fire... Cannot sleep at all.

He tells her there are dreams, which, for him are a continuance of experience, a serialisation of memory like a re-encounter of what should have been. A second chance. Sometimes there are these strange creatures waiting for him, like the patience of stars. But neither does he want. He is old, a sexagenarian. For so long he ate Fungus before sleep. They keep him away (someone had told him). For a time. Then they fight back like malaria finding resistance to an age-old drug.

Yet the flames, somehow, they were real. Never certain of these dreams.

Just memories of brushing leaves now.

There are often words and rhymes which you remember like the need for love and affection, but cannot fathom its meaning nor existence. The mute girl, sitting opposite him, her place at the lintel of its entrance – was good at this. Her quietude preserves them.

LoudCracker.

She names him this because she likes the sound and the word. The fat meaning. Named after village liars. Men who used to say apples grew in November, used to be good at rendering a stale tale to a blowing gale. A "LoudCracker", this eloquent and irrational wind of the wild. But she has always loved this breed of eccentricity, felt safe and accepted somehow. Liar or storyteller, it was the same. Friendly, approachable, ludicrous when in despair. Never lacking things to tell. But above all else liars tolerated people, consumed every whisper of information and insult or name calling with the mild indifference of a block of wood. She herself has never believed nicknames meant anything. Not when one has lived since birth among them.

Near dusk she moves on BMX bicycle to a secret rendezvous. Among and within the hills marked by Gurkhas which appear like spaghetti. A basket and a song and a secret friend, as if floating on unbroken play. Easing through a bounce of shadow. Under a velvet covering of birds she could smell the odour of burnt leaves which the old man almost daily attends to since his secret arrival. There she sees darkness within a void, a silhouette pool. She stops, watching for movement. Nothing. She knew this area well. A forest and a school cocooned by leaves. Her old school, her first school. The darkness of a dusty classroom. She has not been in for years, not since it closed a decade ago and Master Wong bid the village goodbye and gave her the spare key on his way out. She was the last person to see him go. Upon the tired village road adjoining the road to the city he had met her. The heat dampened but still inflamed. She saw his white vest had already wetted through his shirt. Such a conservative man, with spectacles. With hands on her shoulder, kneeling, he buried the key within her fingers. Give this to Uncle Wu, he instructed. But she knew what he meant anyway. Wiping around his neck again he left her. Left her the water mark of his sweaty hand. Walking into the hum of a distant water pump. She waved behind him. But he did not look back. Another hum soon entered the arena of the present hum. She hears it stop impatiently like a growl. The haze of shapes and heightened tones always around her. No movement. No time. She could not see him anymore. Only the purr of machines. An engine rattling off and Master Wong gone, perhaps forever. Leaving her silent predilection for him. For she knew he had a name too. Behind his back they used to call him "Dirty Worm". But in whispers and fear. A classroom of revolving fans which gassed you into sleep. "Crazy Girl, Asylum Woman," voiceless - she could never deflect these names or return the skirmish of an insult. If Wong had been near he would stop them. But he was gone, so were the names, the nudges and the shuffle of whispers behind her. Dogs hounding her. Trucks coming and going with horns so shattering it made her heart jump. Until she reached silence. Among blades of weed and the skims of light. No movement. No time. Her sculptural expression changed only as the laziness of the sky changed. Standing there with nothing in mind and letting everything fill her. And now Wong is gone – his authority. It was the beginning of an end. No one left to school, to educate and play. Even the famous vigil of Gurkhas were going. It was going to be just her and a handful of old widows. A village enclosed by hills and fading ridges. The nicknames were disappearing like the way people would disappear. And one day among the unspoken reclamation of nature she will miss names, miss each wall as they collapse, miss people and their vulgarity. She will miss presence. In the company of shadows she will look for movement or an animal or stones of memory. She is learning to befriend whatever possible visitor there may be in this village of ruins.

Often when he is feeling drowsy he wanders around what is now an adopted space. Always with a broom in his rugged hands and walking within and entering back into honeycombs of shadow which he had previously arrived by. Cleaning, combing, uncovering the yellow baked earth of debris and dead leaves and insects which he knows no one will walk on except her. He knows about her home; this land ruled by the English, knows its various bays and militarised outposts which could do little during the Japanese invasion of December nineteen forty one. But now among this village enshrouded by clean hills, feminine contours, all things come to a stop; vehicles, people, wind and sound. A dead end. Yet a beautiful retreat, he will salute farewell. A place of goodbye, he believes, but that was about all he believes. He has been betrayed enough. As a near sexagenarian he is tired, unthinking, tired of walking. Sleepless. Homeless. He simply needs to sit. A holy room to simply hide. As a beggar he is asking very little.

It was hard just sitting around a shrine at night and occasionally being among animals surfing for scraps. Ghost or man. Surrounded by fortified ruins it was the defensive place against the invisible and madly physical of the elements. Doors that were assigned to remain eternally open, without question, with rides of dust, but with guardians in mind who were now gone, defeated by mortality. The place slightly overrun by lizards and a sand wasp. The cicadas singing in the background. Sometimes a cuckoo's echo. A mute girl traversing its wreckage finding holy shelter away from a world in which she does not belong. Feeding her brood of wild cats colonising among the Ancestral Hall, almost living at the forgotten shrine. Her secret rendezvous with these tiger descendants who allow no human touch. No affection. Until she found him. The man with no name. No past. No need of sleep. Only a blooded footpath of prints. Sitting outside her old school with his left foot bleeding through his white soles. His dumb expression.

Is there no school today?

She ignored him, hearing only the chilly clatter of bamboos. She had ridden into the village only to bury more seeds, hide them as usual within the entangled shadows of the forest and wait for life, as if a slow spell. She had never expected to find this old man, like a lost uncle. His blood prints leading north almost dried. She did not know how long he had been there. She started tearing at her own T-shirt below the waist. Wrapping it round and round his foot like the way her grandma did years ago when she got careless with a hoe. Taking him by the hand to her shrine amongst devastation. But he was not limping. He looked tired, she thought that he may have been dying. So much blood. To leave the world still muttering, like a Buddhist monk. And a sacred place as departure would be good for his soul. So she took him there, lit some incense for his propinquity of death, stole some buns and tofu for prayer, as they do by tradition. Sat with him and waited. But then again he never departed. No. She was glad. She had found a friend.

This village fitting him as if a sarcophagus. The old man felt proud to end in a place of every man's dream. The Chinese dream. The soul that had inspired his peasant logic, the words that no cowherder could ever imagine while brushing school yard leaves or emptying the ashened latrines. There was a desire for knowledge even in the bullish voice of a mainland sexagenarian. There was after all places laid open to his slow understanding.

Each new year a different person was assigned to the care of ChooTong. But there was only the mute girl, a silent wanderer who did not even live there.

Hollow interiors and arms of branches isolate around him. Entrances and bulb sockets empty. Broken tea pots and smashed chairs lay like ravages of war. Solar streams forever spearing them between roofs flooded and collapsed and rotted by rain. The occasional chained door, hiding only splintered secrets. Such a terrace of ruins oscillates his everyday waking. Once a parade of people and animals. Unacknowledged now. Nobody except him. A guest, a Hakka. Invited by the speechless child. There was a huge crack, descending at a diagonal within the walls of the shrine. He often felt a desire to draw, adding there an opposite diagonal so it would take the shape of a Pyramid - which eventually he will. But he had no paint. No instant-whip memory. Just a few yuans.

Always there is the music of cicadas around them. She would bring his rice at noon and dusk. This man with a colonial hat; her responsibility. Who had floated into a deserted village like the Ace in a pack of cards.

Amerrh, he groaned. While she tugs at his arm. Ay? *What?* You love wild things don't you? *They?* I shall. I shall. One day I will tell you about them. Soon. Ha-ha-have not much appetite recently. Must be the heat.

She reaches out and touched his frontal lobes.

Nay! Don't touch. Not that.

He asks her if she has brought him any matches.

During nights of the full moon he is never tired. A habit of work, a haunted past. So many nights awake under the universe of another land, with explosions and flashes. Pre-Buddha. Before the time of dancers. Scraping at a concealed door full of cracks, the last door. Not knowing what moonlight was, no voices, only the encompassing darkness and the clip of his chisel. Repeating his words in Russian. Trying another new language or a poem in mandarin. Radios he found out didn't work under so many tons of earth. Such density of monsoon above him. Such loneliness.

Now under the loneliness of a new space he could recall there was no help, no one around him to cry for help. The girl's cry. Her cry intermingled with a cat's growl. The approach of wild dogs or the old boar which he had come to recognize by its threatening sniff. In the pre-morning darkness he would fake sleep and suddenly sense an awe of presence. Someone, a thing. As he moved his head between the blankets and the stone entrance there would be a loud gallop. Then silence again. Giggling, he knows his early visitors well. And now sitting here, oblique and irrational. His British hat shielding his fragile skull where documents of self endeavour had suffered head on collision, where the nutrition of voices was as important as the food from begging. He waited for death.

He had come by foot (of that he is certain) through dark wet spaces. But warm and painless. Like a beggar. A man who some days within his Autumn life had lived in tombs longer than he lived within sunlight. Darkness is just a game, he knew. And he knew no fear, never scared of deep forest or the quietude of ponds, of warnings etched upon deeds. He often tells the girl he has foreign blood. *Australian – why I am fearless!* At Xuzhou he had witnessed them excavate Han remains but leave the actual sarcophagus untouched. In Suchuan there were river burials architecturally cut into hillsides, into the highest places, behind pines and forgotten under ferns. But times were changing. Building and park developers would inauspiciously find themselves among ancient burial grounds. Providing other opportunist thieves don't get there first. He often speaks of a sarcophagus which measured about thirty feet long. But as usual the tomb had been pillaged and nothing remained. Only legends. Many Books of Creation tell Giants were the first to walk the Earth. Their footprints can still be found in rivers and lakes, in the enhancement of moonlight. So he has been to places. Among belly of curses which frighten men. Ordinary men. Not like him who fears nothing. This violating of a tradition of three thousand years which never anticipated the awful concept of this western science.

Through the village's somnolence, vans now and again throttle in the mirage distance. The Japanese-made Toyota, exclusive to Hong Kong, marked green in stripes for use in the New Territories. They come like clockwork somewhere in the distance. You can hear them. You may with patience and a good ear know who gets off by how long it stops. LoudCracker never sees them. It whirls off again. It's evening.

They are so far away.

He saw no life there, just deserted ruins. Playless. Nothing but staggered remains of children's departure. Vines and monkey bars. Nothing but the occasional explosion of a nearby quarry or the delirious shoulder tapping of casual ghosts – those returning for dollars or those asking for deliverance to other worlds; your world, and steal a ride upon your time, your conscience reality in a fated yet precious life.

Only a village of jars, collective nothingness. Deep dark holes into another universe. There are derelictions that have roofed and kept them. Sealed behind giant doors. Once daily utensils, now secret echoes.

A man with no name. A nickname. A man with no wife. No previous life, ending his last days there. A past figure from over the fence, collected and claimed by innocence. He was here at last, accompanied only by a mute girl near evenings or the occasional sand wasp. They were the only eyes to know he exists among a shelter of holiness.

There were jars of immense diameter, enough to hide a calf. There are jars hunched up inside forgotten spaces in fright. Hollow ceramics of no light. Neolithic jars, with diagrams of spiritual communion. Some jars of music still play those aeolian tunes, strung and whispered through cracks and splinters. Buried among walls and windows. Weeping sounds, like women eternally crying.

There are also jars of bones; human bones, those that have gone before those that have gone abroad. A hill of jars. But bitter, angry contents because of descendants who failed to administer filial aftercare. Such lack of care without proper interment. No soil, no earth, no return. Angered of being just bare bones inside bland jars. The forgotten souls whipped by wind and soaked from rain. Could do nothing while precious land fought over many centuries of pain and regret are sold off forever to rubbish dumps and insatiable power stations.

No one cares, now. It's another dead place.

Only the old could sympathise, like LoudCracker.

Land over there is worth more than respectable burials, he will say. Giggling. But she will know better, see into his smile and know this anger, be accustomed to its need of release.

She comforts him by handing him a bowl of tea. She nods, cares for him, for the stray cats. The mute girl who lives in the distance. He does not know where. Only her feline presence suddenly sliding beside him, sometimes almost rubbing her head on his left shoulder, as if she felt she owned him.

Some days they wander the village together. If not her old school where she found him it will be under the Longans, by the Gun Tower. Upheld as a giant, each face possessing one window, like an eye, the cyclops. She moves away from the huge structure, tugging him away not wanting him to go. But instead he moves toward it. She is like an unwilling horse. *Don't go!*

I have been there anyway, he says. Another barrel of dusts. I am an old man. I am interested in such things, you understand. Iron doors. Settled air, dust and gas... a forgotten breath thousands of years before. Where I found the collectives of immortal elixir of dead kings. Dead creatures which the ancients believed prolonged existence. They were not much different to what we believe today. I know. I had travelled far down the Mekong once. A river farther than life. Toward that exploding light. Toward *them.*

She nods. The mute girl nods as if she could hear, could understand him.

A dog begins barking somewhere. The echo dreamily stretched as if it were resounding in a corridor. In a virginal valley.

The Gun Tower stands adjacent to the main road like the long neck of a spy. It peers over a roof, a series of trees and the haze of a pubic landscape. It is the tallest landmark beside the encircling shoulder of hills. A statement of power which intercepts the eye as you approach, the wordless cyclops. In earlier times, in the beginning when ancestral ashes were smuggled as a motif of faith, careful clusters of community settled and tamed the earth long before they fought wars over opium, long before islands and new territories were claimed. Rice, soya beans, peanuts, pig and duck cries occupied areas of intense human activity. Roads were strange, ghost-like snakes that hardly came or took people anywhere. It was a slow and painful existence. Its settlers were mostly Hakka, a race of communal dwellers. And whose walls still tell you, when injured or pierced by weather, it was built from the bed of opulent rivers.

There are buildings that have through less turbulent times grown away from fortification. Terraces. Leaving the main cell. Such bold moves were mostly headed by homecoming expatriates who appeared on a white horse. But grandeur as such was reflected more than a century ago when the countries they entered only left them feeling ostracized, longing for their cradle of birth. A place where they knew it would be good to spend the last days of a traveller's life. Just waiting. Like the old man nick-named LoudCracker who has spent most of the evening staring into the main road, the only road in or out of his present isolation. Watching the ripple of banana trees huddled among the road. And to him that was also where she comes, a silence of flight.

He sits and seems to live for nothing else but her company and her flasks of tea. Always upon the fallen tree and just near enough within the cool of shade. His thighs almost tickled by the roots which were torn savagely one February night. And now across a road is where it will stay. Forever. Yet somehow there was still life, still photosynthesis, still young fruits as if it too knew the ways of adaptation. With branches outstretched to heaven like a gesture of need.

The tin cup always inserted in his palm at about half past one. Then the bowl.

They wander the fort's dereliction at evening. A warm light pivoting above them and shrivelled structures loosely clinging beside them. Cats begging in the background. She answers them like a mother, but they seem to not know her. He moves to her in-between flowers and shrubs and sudden corners of greenery, silence clinging to his thick forearms which are scarred by burns. His knuckles remoulded. He tells her the name of each flower. Pavetta, Four O' Clock, Yard Grass. Pavetta is used in the case of heat stroke and hepatitis. Dianella and Goat's Horn are for rats and enemies. Every now and then he needed to sit, mostly under the shade of a tree so that there was a breeze as if he needed to dislodge his hat. Old carts and slabs of granite remain idly along the village road which lead west into the city. They would crouch down beside them. She often did this before he came, before the afternoon explosions of a nearby quarry and the vanishing of people. She thinks of the old lady who gave her water melons under this shade. She remembers her one gold tooth and her bony cheeks. Light incinerating the young Longan fruits. Dog barks, echo after echo, song after chatter. She would ask her something then smile. Then scratch under her breast. Then more sounds, more grunts of a motor wearing thin in the air. People, coming home. A laughing dove, like the one singing now. A necessary sound. A family, an echo of wander. There are moments which at times seem to bring back the dead. A string of cries, every now and then in the flush of dusk fall. She looks at the old man again. Nothing. She found him amongst nothing. Except only she knows he is everything. His presence filling a great space. His tutelage of a place cared for by her since the last widow departed to another space. His giggly, unbitter voice, knowing of wind and of darkness. In the dim distance between her destination and the forgotten road and the vanished flicker of his crackling fire.

She turns on the tap. Standing under the old mango she waits. The light is gone. Dark forms filling up corners and particular windows like the water that is going to fill her empty flask. A strange movement suddenly slips above her. Just a feeling, a magpie, she thinks. She sees nothing. The branches being dead still, except for the chorale of cicadas testing the loose air like a lizard's tongue. She turns the nozzle more. Suddenly the *throttle!* and the *sputter!* The only alien sound. Soaking her hands and sprayed down onto her naked thighs. Her shorts wet, but she could hardly see this. Only the feel, the cool, the knowing of spring water channelled from the darkened valley. Again she rinses out more tea leaves. The water omitting such din and so she leaves quickly. Her sandals making another different sound. Moisture. As if there were still people around. But she moves like the evening now, swift and away, past the obfuscation of the Gun Tower.

EMERALD DIARY

IN THE MIRROR SHE APPEARED as an emergence of beige. Sometimes in spectacles. Sitting alone, a cool face in uniformity, a camouflaged silence. The serene roar in a warp of images flooding beside her. She is bathed in a light of the late at the rear, the farthest depth of a shuffling vehicle which occasionally swerves viciously round deepening bends. Nothing disturbs her. Her head arced, searchingly, into a play of mountains the vehicle now seems irrevocably heading into.

Where are you going?

For a while there is no answer. No reaction. Where are you going? asks the driver. Voices, as if wanting to be immune from them. She moves over toward the face of the minibus and tells him the name of the place. What? Are you sure? He turns again, checking the youthful certainty of her plain contours, her baggage already slung behind herself, ready to alight. Is someone meeting you there? *Are* you sure?

The minibus which can capacitate fourteen hurls further into the rural sparseness like a battling boulder. At moments she might find herself aligned against the border and the mediaeval barricades or sway past huge baskets or corroding carts of spring onion. China only a hand's distance away, crowned by razors of wire butting the burning sky, where the hip of a mountain may suddenly evolve or may gradually fade from a haze of blue sleep. Such mellow vision. The reclined nature of village hills or the still life of baskets left by the roadside. A fade of smells. Long ago now. What she can remember as a child.

Nobody lives there anymore. You know that? Nobody. She remained composed against the window. The vehicle taking the right on the Y fork. She tells him she was going in. Staying a night or two. Now? On your own? But nobody lives there...

She turns away from the voice. Light stroking a cluster of hills. No sign of life. An expression reflected by the glare of glass. This territory of reflection. Arrived halfway around the world. In between education. Beige. This was all her. The meaning of being away from home. Being somewhere on one's own impulse. This was a spirit who loved cities, enjoyed the commotion of things where after school she would sneak into washrooms of Covent Garden and undress and reappear with a friend as anything but uniformed. She always loved the noise, the level it progressed. Musical chaos. While silence remained an obeisance. She, a silent soul. Quietude in her thoughts and movement. Why, noise and colour was something she never had but perpetually needed. The colours of experience even if sometimes it meant silence. Like the village now that is ahead. Looking more and more like gauze through the glass. Through into another reality.

What did you say your Aunt's name was? Right. Yes, I remember her. Passed away about two years ago. I know many people in the New Territories. In this job that's natural. Where did you say you're from? England? How long have you been away?

The engine purr was at times deafening. She was almost there.

The place has been deserted more than a year now. Have not driven into the area for months. The last time was them rushes of overseas relatives coming back in response of the lands. You know it? That's right. Lucky pilgrims aren't they? The government buys their ancestral land and they fly away dollars happier. They don't stay long. I drop them off and pick them up the same day. Things like this have been the norm in places like Sai Kung. Some say it's the ravage of the land and burials. I say good luck to those who benefit. They come, sign some papers and they are never seen again.

You're still serious about staying *there*? Why not come back tomorrow?

The vehicle comes to a halt around a syphon of willows. A door releasing her into them, a mellow glow and a sudden hesitation. She begins to alight.

Listen, I'll wait for you. Can't drive in because of a tree fallen during the last storm. I don't trust a young girl in this area after dark. I'll be here for ten minutes. O.K.?

She turns from him, feeling uneasy about his concern. The engine silenced now. She is standing beside an iron billboard. A dark skeleton. She reads what is still available after the rain and heat and the wind. The English alphabet mauled and dried like dead elephant skin.

> ...All concerned : (Claims) Please contact The Lands and
> Tribunal. Fanling, New Territories.

A road. Gun Tower. Now and again the wail of some strange creature. This figure within the ease of Longans. The vehicle is out of her vision now. Moments later to be away from them all, wrapped in the atmosphere of evening she enters. Its surface so clean and kept it seemed somehow the place had been previously swept. Emerald in her office clothes, she could not appear more out of place. Her steps raucous in the air but timid when landing, as if aware of ones disturbance, ones past. Under the shadow of birds slipping between the whistle of branches, she arrives at the tap by a tree. The earth damp. Scatters of water the colour of sky, dried colours. For a while she waits here, attempting to smell the darkening membrane which is filled with noises and cries invisibly hung from towering branches. The recurrence of memory. A map of childhood. It was all here somewhere. A school perhaps or a forest she knew, where within, somewhere in its disowned chaos is possibly a saint, an avuncular deity and many trees as old as the migrated saint himself. Through the darkness. No movement, no order of identifiable form.

For a while she waits here. Feeling the weight of her shoulder sack. The rustle under the leaves until she hears a sudden roar, a disturbance. *Duhht! Duhht!* After which there was tranquil silence. Nothingness.

She turns to look, whipping up her dark hair in the motion of an arc. But saw only the tunnel of trees from which she had just emerged. A choral and chaotic breeze, a surface as if previously hand-swept.

She turns away again, hearing nothing more of the vehicle that had moments ago transported her desires and taken her identity and ran with her from the smell and restless tide of a city.

Now, darkness of buildings begins to surround her. This corner of isolation. Perhaps it was what she wanted. She is truly alone in a place of memory. The wind rasps through a holy corridor of leaves.

It is like a play world, the evening glow. She unlocks a groaning door out of a terrace of abandonment, finding damp everywhere. The crest of noise filling unbroken spaces. The breathless rooms lay idly through the door which she has opened. Light glimmering on the floor. Inside there is an interior Monsoon, where Aunt Gao had left it as if she would return, like clues to her lonely existence. She can smell the decay of moisture as she penetrated the room's spareness. There is a staircase, an upper void of a dark universe. She stops at a table centred within the darkness. She picks up a candle normally used in ceremonies. Lights it. Stands there with it against the colourless wall not knowing why it is colourless until she sees photographs. She steps up toward it, soon finding herself.

During the months here she would spend long periods simply gazing at herself. The pampered frock and her guardian of an angel, the black and white. There were many items which could send up memories, cause a standstill or flood her with nocturnal company. The red flasks against measly walls were still there. Cold tea on hot days, occasional afternoon slumbers, awaking and searching. Aunt Gao always at the tap washing cabbages, preparing the day's last meal as if she were still alive, still lighting a lantern.

She would touch nothing until the next day. There was a sacredness of objects because of the evening. Only the stove fuelled by butane gas for some tea or the crackle of her portable radio. Otherwise, there was not a soul. And that was when she came. The mute girl.

Near darkness. As the girl in beige colour began thinking about the driver of the minibus. Who are you meeting there at this hour? *Who?*

Is it you? She muttered. It really *is* you!

The silhouette reticent by the huge doorway flatly shook itself.

She runs over to collect her visitor's hand, reaching out, sprayed like star fish. Pulling themselves into a mist of artificial light and into their frozen reunion. A friend near dusk, a meeting with silence, a rambling soul who does not speak. Only a corroded mutter.

Oh, say something you dumb pooch! It's me. May! Can't you see I am glad to see you?

The mute girl shrugs.

May...

Somehow she is unsure of the bright voice. The feathery way in which she has drifted in. From a time before you knew pubic hairs could sprout.

Not a bit! You have not changed! Still not a word. I used to think when you grew up you might be able to talk, supposedly like how a butterfly colours itself.

A visitor is always distracted by the excitement of atmosphere around them. Preoccupied in new senses. The questions, the arrangements. They are somehow blinded by sheer excitement.

The mute girl heaves at the twin doors, sealing away the night. It seemed she had come all the way to do this, slotting the bolts into place and staring silently at May's every move.

Outside. Darkness ascends into the valley. In a flutter of stars.

A pair of slippers, *flip flops*. What she exchanged for the city. When she awoke again the following day among the chorus of birds, it was almost noon. She found herself on the old settee, the one with light upholstery and flowers where she slept near midday aged four or five when the summer heat omitted nothing but somnolence. She sees her silent friend at the stove. Her tresses are in a simple pony tail. She yawns and reaches out for her glasses. So she never left her last night, sleeping perhaps on the sun stretcher now lying beside her, collapsed and folded. It was she who dug out an old blanket and covered her while she laid there. She had fallen away upon that childhood surface, a candlelight spraying in the darkness, in rippling shadows. And slept without even knowing.

Now, before her, lay a neat pair of flip flops, probably once belonging to her Aunt. She slipped into them just as she did the way she slipped hypnotically into a village. Tea was smuggled towards her as the radio twitched nervously into life. Later she slipped into trousers.

What is the time? Why didn't you wake me?

It was a deep sleep. The kind that staggered between sudden consciousness. Somewhere among her dreams a shout had hauled her up. A repetitious pinch. The crow of a cock at dawn.

A decision is a decision. That was her character. She had left the office without a note and equivocally slid down onto Gresson Street then Johnston Road. The traffic now and again tamed through the afternoon light. In the damp echo of buses. She is swift on and off them, her grey skirt hardly touching the seat or anybody who she might pass in her departure out of the city. Once across the harbour she catches another bus from Nathan Road. Carnarvon Road. Chatham Road. Home. She is never relaxed.

The phone was ringing a long time. There are photographs of three people eating at a table. A trio of young women, their habits leaving a book on the table or a stocking under a cushion. Each room was lined modestly in posters, teddy bears and dried roses. They are all out except one. She looks out of the window to see if there is the possibility of rain. Then she turns off the radio. There is no time to change. She swiftly takes the shoulder sack and moves from her room. She is always rushing. The phone still ringing.

She looks back. What have I forgotten? Stares for a while at the sound hanging on the light blue wall. They must know. Her brother must know – someone must have seen her leave work. But she won't pick it up. Not for the authority of a god nor saint. She leaves the room, leaving a note on the table in front of the photographs. Slamming the door then the iron gate. She does not wait for the lift and descends the stairs. Turning, spinning, she cannot think. But she had to leave. Get out of the city. The voices, her parents' authority permanently looming over her. That damn phone!

What, are you mad?

Yes. I am mad.

She is down on the street, down and awoken by turbulent reality.

They turn over the bedding, drying them under a spy of light. The Mute coughing under the flare of dust. The Gun Tower hazily outlined beyond them.

Oh, yes. Who is he?

Not illegal is he? A Snake?

The Mute neither nodded nor agreed. Still oddly shy even in the presence of a long ago friend, an older sister, sometime guardian. Someone who levelled with her, picked her up off the dirt of names. No nicknames. This most unusual of person to befriend who always wore a dress immediately after school, colourful after dark. But who would not hasten to lash out at faces which tore at her hair or wrote callous names in the mute girl's text book. A big sister who has somehow suddenly and for a reason returned. From noises and dust, for *her* perhaps.

In a faded sky, in a courtyard of stones she would move as if checking for order. And she, the silence would follow, xerox her, carefully watching her every step near dead twigs or near dead snakes or when she is too close near the crumbling wreck of the Gun Tower. She had watched the city girl and knew things were diluted. Scarcity of images, without the clarity of her own silence which preserves so well. A reach or a clasp and she would be near. Assure her it was nothing. A harmless creature - a Gecko lizard, the carcass of a flung out snake killed by the brood of stray cats. Kraits and vipers and the occasional butterfly. The oddly savage remains of a previous night hunt – possibly out of pure instinct or habit rather than hunger. To kill or be killed. Caretakers of the Ancestral Hall.

Who is that man?

She looks at her. They were approaching the old well. She nods. Among the swirl of more aeolian bamboos the silent girl had been expecting it. Questions. But not so soon.

In the thelt of darkness of last night; his fire, his toothless smile. May had caught the scent of smoke as she passed after the vehicle had gone. The main road which continued through and slowly dies in a sharp right. A courtyard then a path over a pond. His fire had alerted her. So the shock was elusive. A man and a fire. Senselessly sedentary among the ruins, counting, seven, eight. Nine. Cats among ruins. Nothing but cats. Their territory. For a while she could only stare at them. He had said, in a quaint chuckle, he was somewhere from beyond. A colonial barrier that used to be a mystery. The English, the Sikhs, the Scottish, the Gurkhas, who patrolled there. Kept runners away, midnight refugees, people like him, this incognito man. *Be careful! Don't walk there!* There were no questions. Just that cracked smile. Harmless old thing mumbling in Hakka dialect in a place where supposedly there was not a soul.

Where did he get all those wild cats from?

Oh, you feed them. I see. You feed him as well.

She gazes at the allotment in front of the terrace. The density of it. Full of brambles dispersed and sheds imploded like a secret garden, or simply a place to hide.

I will wake here, she said. Wake until everything else around me is clear and uncovered.

The Mute girl turns to her, as if she understood, as if she could speak.

Silence near evening. She strolls alone now. Pure and without a soul. She moves under a forest gate and enters beyond into a playground. Watching her reflection slip along the mood of school windows. The chairs and table motionless within them, partly left, abruptly organised. The past months of eating out over chairs and tables with a man she thinks as a friend, a trustee, known many years and known well to her family; her four brothers. In the Art Deco smudge of Ophelia Café he dined her, almost touched her, trying; wanting to know her. Understand the fire which he seems to have fallen in love with.

He would wait at the usual table by the street window. She was always late.

Come to Malaysia. There are better prospects for you.

But she would always laugh it off. And he, uncertain whether she was amused or angered at his daily insistence, sipped his tea, pushed forward his plate, the soft music wailing, looked away then wiped his mouth. He was cautious of her quick temperament.

Why not? Your parents agree. And I will be around. Think about it. No need to rush.

His hair neatly parted, handkerchief lay in his breast pocket. It was what she liked about him most. The ridiculous order. The lawyer. You could guess exactly what he was. Could not appear casual even if he tried. Name and power and finance, all these she learnt from him. What it could offer as the Asian dream. But there was also this meticulous care and kindness which she knew only of him. The opening of a door or the retraction of her chair. So gentlemanly. This man who has asked for her hand.

No rush.

There was a vicious row. Mother. First brother. She could not remember who had started it. Because mother had always spoken well of him. In fact the entire family was in absolute favour of him. Daniel Ng. Because of his insistence. The family insistence of him against her. He is speaking in your best interests. What, are you mad? They would not stop. It was breaking her. Arrows coming from all directions. The man who had three years ago when she was at High School accompanied her into London to see the Picasso Retrospective.

I am not marrying him because you say so!

She put down the phone and minutes later left the room. She was a person who if troubled, will run with the wind.

In the arboreal place. Always smouldering leaves near a school. White smoke now and again in blinds of light or the call of unknown birds now and again near darkness. The singular explosion at evening. A fire and the old man. An awaiting friend. Somewhere in the distance lurked a figure slowly easing toward all this. Who celebrated in silence all beginnings of sacred life.

She moved and repositioned herself in mysterious ways. A cup or a sacred statue or the emotional wandering of a human being. The girl of silence returns timely near the transition of echo. Sits at the earthenware like some long gone guardian. Closing the obese doors. Her stare without quiver in the candlespray. In a world of her making there was nothing she was unfamiliar with. Not insect nor visitor nor the odd night trespass. Not the owl behind the forest nor the crack of a twig in the furnace would stop May at the night table but which she absorbed with minimal hesitancy. During these nights just staring at the back of her friend who sat writing. No dialogue. She will know happiness was alive. Perhaps temporarily. No promises. Only her horoscope of senses like the way she knew of propinquity of nightfall or the hunger of wild cats, who feared no darkness and no serpents but feared her. Loving them for no other reason than simply the love she sees in them. Like the old man or for May. Creatures who when knowing of her presence gave nothing less than their attention and the look of a face. A face facing her and not the back as if deflecting or ignoring a curse hoping it may sooner or later go away.

Like a wall. The back of a person.

A veil.

Am I dying? She thought. No dialogue. No faces.

Faceless. A back. Strangers or parents. Their backs were turned to her. Always the talkless back facing her. Deflecting an unwanted child. Misconceived. The menstrual blood was difficult to clean. Still bleeding. Stained. All she really needed was words then, a cuddle or the comfort of scolding. No matter who. Why am I bleeding? But she was a shadow after all, a bird no one ever bothers noticing. Part of the pastoral scenery – there to be taken advantage of when in silence or when there seems no one is watching. And for a while the injury seemed all hers and nobody else's.

Until she found him that is. A tired face.

The bleeding old man.

The 1967 post dynastic assault of Hong Kong Sovereignty left nothing but a wall of fear. Framed with metal. Silence between two lands. The stir of a Middle Kingdom shaken of its cultural senses. There was no more filth. No more newspapers blown over by accident. No more intellectuals.

It was a time of National Service. The terrorism of Homemade Pineapples. A period of beggary corpses washed loosely down from the Pearl River Delta. An exodus of faces where among each bush, each valley, each boulder by the sea had its own story of tragedy. Individuals and families running from a great nation. That's if snakes and sharks had not already met them first.

There are village notions of Tseun and Wai. Meaning Cluster and Fort. The latter an ancient defence against the notoriety of bandits and Pacific piracy. Kaw Lui, Chuk Yuen, Heung Yeun, Lin Ma Hang. Such migration of faith and the yielding of new land. A road entering all this. A life line, a corridor of divided lands where the sound of water will carry a passenger through oases of metal and abandoned gravestones which point the way eastward into a chain of soft ridges. Chicken shacks and endless barriers and the swamp of serpents. Then nothing. A climb. A beautiful drop. The Pak Kung Au ridges. The occasional remains of roofs and sudden windows and forgotten suggestions of reworked earth perhaps. Lizards and wild porcupines swarm there. Only the shadow of cranes now. A corridor designated as Military Use. A trade route of the ancient going to the sea.

There is evidence of caves a hundred yards prior to this solitude. Geological legacies. Nostrils of darkness housing a rare species of bat protected by law and guarded by superstition. Once a well of minerals and people and carts of earth. A tunnel, some still say. Rumours of a subterranean passage into China from which many have not returned. Into places light has never reached since creation.

And so there are days this man from beyond would talk of a river. The subterranean river. Not sure whether dream or underworld. Not certain whether he is still dreaming now among the ruins and the presence of youth.

There was a fragrance. A murmur of breeze. Which did not prescribe hell. For so long he could see nothing. Not a wink of light. Bare footed. Lizards moving around him. Rocks sliding before him. The sudden aerosol of bats. *'Darkness and liquid and passages are baptisms of a new beginning...'* wrote the Great Hermit after climbing back up again from death of his tomb. LoudCracker had felt immortal only once. An ephemeral lease of a special race whose power radiated the blasting nights. The offer of escape. A river of primates. A superior race. And for a while he flowed with them. Supposedly like now.

Datura? Pavetta? Yes. Jade Orchids. He follows the fragrance. His naked sole feels the jagged rocks and crevices. Man's implementation. Leftover of pick axes and some rib cages of rusting support. He feels the terrible sharp pain as a broken clam digs up into his bare flesh. The sting when bleeding in water. But he cannot see. There is no light. Just early ideas of a step. A stairway of turbulence. Sensual draft like release. Endless trails of corrosion and collisions with soft creatures. But he could see nothing. No colour of red or the feel of blood. And then the stench of bat dung. Dried. Heaven still black for such a long time. But somehow the perfume is stronger as if just above the next step. The smell like food caressing his hollow belly.

At last the aerosols of light. An exit of stone upon the aftermath of warmth. He emerged bleeding into the light. Half encircled by this yellow fragrance. He has come out of the womb.

There was no electricity. Not a wink of road lamps. All power was cut after the village was declared derelict. So almost every night they saw their way with candles. Old candles used for worship. Even encasing paper lanterns that they had found over the flame, dangling them on a rod and moving playfully around in the darkness. There were locations which they would leave a particular light, the darkest corner or a wet cubicle such as the wash area which was situated near the door where a head level wall keeps the secrecy of bathing. Before May could wash, her friend would firstly check for frogs and things which might have crawled through the drain and squatted on the concrete seat which the unsuspecting user will need to sit on. They transferred hot water from the huge wok of the earthenware, burning each night. Dried branch and thicket crackling in the miniature furnace, only hours ago gathered by them from the shallow of woods behind the terrace.

She would wake and find her gone. Returning always at noon with the basket for the man and his brood of cats.

Most days she spent in the courtyard. Letters under the shade because she had forgotten her diary. Beside the tap or the family row of Longans. Roots and concrete and shadow. There she could smell the marshes which lay beyond her like a huge plug within the sink of mountains, where a stream had for hundreds of years flowed down into village life. A field of rice. Ducks. But all she can see now is marshland. And the isolation of telegraph poles.

During the end of each day she would look that way and watch out for signs of Kingfishers.

Why did you leave? A neat fire burning before them. Near her voiceless friend at the old shrine where a sea of cats would scatter like a fallen bomb. No light around them. Nothing else but a camp fire. This old man with no identity. Too tired to run. Who now counts day by day with a broom in his hand. She had wandered into the fort and then into them like the way one would enter for the love of silence. Wanting no disturbance. During these early nights in a deserted village near the Chinese border, writing when raining or buying food in the city when radiant, no plans of contact with civilisation, she seems at peace. Not caring. As if a refusal to grow or a need to hide. The old stranger always giggling at her. A near toothless smile. So informal, yet polite.

"School friends," he kept muttering, "Ay, so you are old friends. Wonderful! I wish I were like you when I was young. Truly now..."

A wail of some bird. Somewhere yet nowhere.

I am mad. She thinks again. They both edge around him. May seeming awkward, ill at ease. Since her friend was harbouring this man in secrecy she had decided to avoid him altogether. Not mentioning another word. Avoid his company of existence.

"W-w-where did you say you were from?"

"England," she replied.

"Yes. Yes. I remember."

"You been there?"

"No." He giggles. "I am old. I cannot go anywhere any more."
Her friend still eyeing out a cat. He does not look at her, but has kept
his attention on the fire.

"What did you do back there?" she finally asked.

He starts to giggle again.

"A man can live a long life sometimes, amoy. Too long! It is a
tough life, *us* Hakka folks ... Tough life." He begins sipping tea.
There is no movement around them. Only the forest behind. Bursts
of shadow over them.

He leans back into the cushion of his own voice.

"A long life. That is all. Too long. Big hands." He laughed,
holding out his rough paws.

"I once castrated bulls with them. Yes. Edible, you know.
Economize. Not like tiger scrotums. I tied the animal to bars of
windows or the trunk of an elm. But a swift snip cannot guarantee
success. I have seen them rip out the wall or realise seconds too late
what has happened then gallop off and never be seen again.
"Billing Borrum! Billing Borrum! Amerrh .... Never seen again.
Cats are different. No struggle. Truly! Always use a water jar and
place them head first into it. Well, they will growl as if saying "Warn
you, I cannot be messed about!" Like a child's marbles. You squeeze
them out. Yet there is not much blood, not like buffaloes.

"But after. No more is it the same animal anymore. The spirit
goes. The famous angry puff. There is nothing left of the powerful
horn. Senile. And people are no different. They too can be broken."

"Yes. But why did you leave?"

"Leave, amoy?" There was a faint chuckle. "Can't die there.
Could not – that's why. The Letter. Envelope of the P-P-Peoples
Seal."

"Ngar me ngy sat-h! I was not permitted a traditional burial it
said. Going to ashes when dead. Like how they rid Enemies of the
People, counter revolutionaries and intellectuals. Not a trace. Not a
last word. Carried into rivers by the detonated wind – all that
intended for me. An old and worthless man – they think!"

"I don't know how they will treat a king confined by eternity. But I ask you – how can a man die with no funeral? Is this all they could offer a Hakka man? After a four thousand year tradition?"

"You know, we were great once. A great empire. Kingdoms of immortality where nothing ever dies."

There is a long pause before he starts to gather up the twig fire. Before he strikes the fire.

"Ay, it can't be helped."

The faces of stone gods had been flickering. The area within the jungle had been demarcated. More than a dozen of PLA troops guarded it. Signs in Cambodian guarded it. No one was supposed to enter. A transfer of property agreed by the Khmer government and they were there courtesy of that truce. Camped around the mouth of the ground entrance of this great discovery. Somewhere back in the past, in a working life.

There were about three men lowering him down using the winch of a Jeep. Unevenly and without light for a few minutes. He was going down diagonally moving in a slow curve. This began briefly always after dusk. The scatter of clouds bare red pasted upon the tall branches. That murmur of the jungle like warning.

His hair always covered with dust by the time he reached the subterranean hallway. The lightlessness and the lack of freshness. First he would light the lamp. Then put on his Topi. And realise he was alone. He throws a halo of agoraphobia around himself. Nothing but alkali feldspar glittery like ripples. Other than that, there is little of interest here, only the bone remains of a thousand year old thief. The repetition of one's own footsteps.

They had arrived during the rainy season when the jungle seemed like the innards of a sea creature. Constant damp. Not good at all for arthritis. Palladius was already there months ago having been obsessed by the excavation. The Hakka man was a replacement of his "late" assistant who died of malaria. "I need someone who is not easily cowed by customs and legends. Curses, I mean. The Chinese of course being traditionally superstitious about such work...." Such work. Archaeology. Compared to the turmoils of the Red Guard years, a sacrilege of death to him, seemed far less sacrilegious than say, that of human life. And he would never forget that. At his age, nearing death. And that reason, the cure for that, was precisely why he was here.

Immortality. The drug. The elixir. The First Emperor could not find it, sent voyages towards Japan to find it. Alchemists in the Seventh century accidentally invented gunpowder in the process of it. Not even modernity could overcome man's desire for it. And then one day in the jungles of Angkhor they found it, supposedly. In a king's tomb.

He stood there every night unbelievably amazed. What an honour – to be among the elliptical room of bottles. Jars. Pillars constructed of individual jars. Hundreds and hundreds stacked upon one another sandwiched between skeletal bronze. A museum of undated lifeform. Unnamed. Palladius estimated six hundred and eighteen. Preserved in a liquid solution of salt and liquorice roots. The contents range from odd collections of insects to small hairy mammals. Through the glow of the Davy lamp he viewed them, guessing at their carnivore period, at their aphrodisiac usage. What great kingdom? What degree of life embalming? Like discovering the missing wishes of life from the genie in a bottle. Light absorbed by the hungry glass, swallowed and throwing back three thousand years as glitters of white.

At first it was understood to be a royal burial. But breaking through into the room of jars altered all prior speculation. There was no sarcophagus, no threnody of carvings nor the evidence of bones. Only the remains of a thief - who was never cunning enough to make it past the second crossbow. It was a slow progression. Most of their time was spent dismantling traps and covering up pressure points which activated pitfalls. A long corridor leading toward something. Murals pre-oriental. Cracks would emerge suddenly for no reason. Pillars were steadily being nudged, growing up into the ceiling. The tomb at times appeared to be moving all over. And any man should know nothing moves in a tomb.

"This is no tomb," said Palladius, who was always scraping away bits of history. His Ukranian ascent undetectable, working under the meshed flame.

"....it's the Elysium of another beginning."

He pokes the fire. The mute girl watches him. Amoy, at my age you get to know the variety of earth. I know the smell between good soil and poison. Give me dry dust and I can tell you that name. The use in life and after. That purple shale you pick around these hills – attractive is it not? Ay, where I was, there is such shale. And if dropped in water it can dissolve like your friend's tablets.

A snarl of noise from the forest suddenly breaks his thought. LoudCracker looks back. Tilting his baggy chin. She follows his gaze.

You had better go now. See if your friend needs you. Then his attention drifts back into the fire. He pokes it again. Sparks rising into a swirling crackle.

He keeps remembering Palladius's linger of words. *"The man before you – said he was consistently troubled by nightmares..."*

"I just ignore them."

Brave words. It was because of the gods. The stare of Angkhor gods. The place of dreams. They made you dream. It was because of obsession. A very old human desire. From the murals in the corridor Palladius deciphered a race of horse people. Chariots. Hunters. Once a mighty empire which spanned the whole of this south eastern continental tip known now as Myanmar, Thailand, Cambodia and Vietnam. In a time when there were Three Great Rivers. A warrior king. Intermittent periods of peace. It was all very interesting. But there was still nothing to suggest the place as a tomb. There were no scenes of death, no declarations of afterlife, no promises of heaven. Until they found the room of jars.

"How can a great race such as this not leave behind remains of themselves? If they believe in God there must be death. But where is God? If they didn't believe in death then must they have the answer contrarywise to death...."

This was how Palladius always spoke. A secular voice in the echo of darkness. Logical and fearless. Like the Hakka man he hired to help chip away the glass contents – believed to be possible elixirs of deathlessness. Three cases had already been smuggled back into China for top analyses. If the Palladius theory was right, the entire room will go. But it all required dexterous handling because of the fragile interior. One false move and they could be buried forever. In a land of civil war two men working together made less error, less unnecessary movement. They would be immune from all chaos of men. So they thought.

It was so far the most peculiar jar he had seen. After two nights he finally cleared it from its bronze holder. Holding it in front of the glow of the lamp. What was it? A lynx? A bat? A monkey? It looked all these things - enshrined in a wonderful egg-shaped jar. He walks clear from the room now. Leaves it altogether and descends a steep stairway in the narrow corridor. Always the echo of each step as if there was someone else, a few thousand steps, thousand hands that built them with fear. Coughing out the dreadful shale dust he arrives at the last step. Sitting and inhaling from the oxygen tank. Careful the jar does not roll down into the darkness next to him. But it was here suddenly that there was movement. He hears movement. Something was wrong. Out of the normal. Nothing had moved for so long. Supposedly a tomb, after all. Distrustfully, he turns his head.

And saw no more the room of jars. A bronze door instead had suddenly alchemized before it, a trap door.

So for a while there was nothing they could do.

"It's false," concluded Palladius. "Corroded mechanism. I think it was meant to be activated many months ago when we first broke through. It's nothing."

But the man with Topi only glared at him. He was familiar with this tone of phrase, the easy dismissal of godspell architects, eager to proceed at all costs. Like this place, at human costs. But now being in each other's unconsciousness of archaic fear; tired, both in the ball of soft light which encapsulated them – there would appear to be no other plausible explanation. And moments later he will leave Palladius. Going back up into the jungle while the Russian continued where he left off. Carefully recording and tediously scraping. *Tap, tap, tap* as he crossed the flimsy suspension bridge they made of climbing rope. The terrible darkness he views below which is depthless. Light simply disappears. Towards more stairs and a longer and less detailed corridor till the tapping appeared less intrusive and more hypnotic. Further away from the room of bottles and jars. The chamber of immortals. This national treasure unclaimed and forgotten in a land of civil war. But he was tired now. Sleep. Just three hours was enough. It would sharpen his old senses again. At this hour of dawn he felt nothing was in place. Not him, not in a foreign land, not in a tomb. Yawning, he inhales the dust – and, something else. What was it? No. *It's nothing.* He needed sleep. After that everything would be clear.

He could see the rope just ahead of him.

There was no sound. The chiselling had suddenly stopped. Palladius has stopped. A long pause. He feels a ticklish suck of air. He ignores it. Then more flutters of dust. He sniffs the air again. Gas? He checks the Davy lamp. Normal. But he feels it again. Something was coming up behind him. He looks behind himself. He starts to run. He looks behind again. He sees the flames. He sees the rope. A fiery embalment.

His dark world suddenly being filled with light.

A book is opened on page 280 on the morning table. There is no one around. A skin of paper beside the mysterious book. A fountain pen and a pair of spectacles.

> Ah-Funn and I went flying home as light as air
> And I carrying the dream of Wuthering Heights,

No school. No adults. For a while in-between the peeling of silence May laid there. This once in her life. It was special here. Light was pouring into her room. The window a loudspeaker of nature. With nothing of the outside world as she lay. Feelings of earth burning under the sun. Light creating music. Bottles of sound. From her friend installing the kettle to the groaning of the giant doors. Like the Book of Genesis. The first movement. The delicacy of the first rhythm. She lay there imagining them. Just the rhapsody of people. I wonder what ever happened to Wet Boots? The man who sold delicious steam? And fish balls. How did the fishmonger create such a wonderful cry? Such haunted cries, she thought. And sprang into the morning illuminance which is the cold floor – half naked looking for her flip flops.

Later, they would follow the evening home. After Sheung Shui, their nearest city. The Mute walking the streets as if a terrified cat afraid of water. Always there is May, the cloak, wrapping her rural nakedness.

They approach the village with long shadows thrown before them. The village road, which carried in and out their ritual privacy was flung over by a savage possession of figs and leaves. Mostly banana leaves dancing coquettishly along the rim of the road. The wind of the valley now and then scattering their loose of hair.

During nightfall they brought the old man fresh food and sat with his cartoon laughter. Sat with flip flops.

He had walked back into her life so casually. There was nothing more than a suddenness found in foxes. A pilaster for his chair. A warmth of voices. He would reconnect her like rain into a river. This can happen. A morning passenger.

Once children together, she now found him among the ruins. Shoeless. Barefooted. Colour of flesh blended with light at the place of worship and sitting across from the old man.

Light falls swiftly here, he kept repeating.

They do not recognize each other. Not yet. Even names were no clues to their ride of infancy together. Only colours, perhaps. The colour of a dress. Only polite words now.

Did you say you were from England?

Yes. Berkshire, you know it?

Berkshire? Well, I am really from Canada. But I was there. For three years at Brunel.

Oh, really...

Yes.

How long ago was this?

The old man sat watching them. Boy meets girl. A smile gradually leaking around his plump features.

Bucolic architecture never believed in doors. Only voids. The only doors were the wooden entrance which was the only exit. There are no rooms. Washing, sleeping, personal privacy occurred behind a billowing curtain. The hypothesis of a nuclear family. The higher the building, the greater the family name, the cooler the summer. Upstairs was more like an extended periphery of the interior. This format of building was standard in Asia. Air circulating around open spaces as freely as a child's voice echoing among the valley walls.

At night the fluorescence of candlelight enclosed them. Dark winds surround them. They were permanently settled downstairs because the city girl disliked the upper darkness which seemed to move and groan during the night. There seemed, with all the crenellation of metal and the bolts of wood, nothing that could enter except mosquitoes and moths. During this time the old man often walked them back. His habit. Manners and warnings.

Every now and again May's friend feeds more twigs into the hearth where it heats the huge earthenware. For a fairy's bathing water. She moves from one corner to another, from one object to another, positioning them in many mysterious ways. She knew about rooms, about people long gone. Had freed herself within them when widows were lonely or when her presence reminded them of some older time. Colourful times. She does not fear the darkness or the lifeless at all. She fears only for her friend. The city girl.

Dearest Yam,

> *There are people you meet near darkness like the radiant knights of a book. They seem strangely mysterious, no traces of the deliriousness of scent, like armour within a more precious armour where the delicacy of a heart can emit a cry. A chime. And I wake, lie awake, to simply and blessedly wake in a surrounding of demure touch, sensing the linen of breeze or caressed by a thief of wind.*

> *Somehow I feel I am being harboured by these things and notions. A friend who is younger than I. Yet older and wiser in this environment I forsook many years ago. Who keeps her silence. Collect her seeds and seasonal bugs and even plucks flowers to place at my bed. We are descendants of a village and of an old school. She does not talk, but I can feel she is there. Know her timid, quirky moves. She has collected an old man somehow. Unwanted or forgotten, an outdated kind of book. Today I saw her collect another man, though younger – about my age. Who are they? Songs whirled deeply around*

*them. One says, have you eaten? One says, he must leave.
How long have they been there?*
*I wish she could talk sometimes, if not all the time. There is
a spiritual essence of silence isn't there? Like this place I've
come to. Holiness. But there is this old man. And now there
is this other man. He is from the city. An expatriate – like me.
He never stays long.*

All evening she had mentioned nothing. Scribbling now and again
from a book of printed words which the wordless girl had not yet
seen. But she couldn't read English anyhow. She never read at all.
Just playing was her desire. Climbing the monkey bars or scaling a
tree. She often did this with someone who was here too. Not so long
ago. An old friend. Today she saw them together. Though May
probably does not know who he is yet. And the Mute won't tell. She
simply moves mysteriously.

During the night they remained within each other's bubble of
candlelight. The glow of paper lanterns. Each other's face flickering
intermittently, changing a smile or a gaze, contours altering every
time the flame faltered. Occasional insects floating close enough not
to be burnt would displace a panorama of shadows of a theatre of
walls. If there are murmurs or lightning or the cry of an owl they will
huddle up together in bed. In the darkness, inside the aerosol of a net.
Pretending they are invisible. Sometimes even by two am they are not
yet asleep. Her eyes bright in the creature-filled moonlight.

Remember Mao? Yes? He lived next door. An evil bastard –
evil man, I mean. Every morning he played those terrible songs. The
Army marches. It was not illegal. *One, two, one,* something about a
badge and Red Flags and preparing to sing. I think altogether there
were nine soldier rules. Don't disobey orders, no alcohol. But the
funniest part was never to liberate pornography! But all the same
there was not a man less liked. When I was ill, a fever. My aunt
begged him to take me to the doctors. It was one of those treacherous
nights when Snakes slipped the borders. There was rain. Thunder.
He was my closest relative.

In the end, uncle Sang who made a living carting men and
commerce took me. He carried me through the rain.

Bicycle in the rain. He carried me through the sound of
shimmering lights.

I've always had visions of being on the back and moving through glimmers. Pain makes you remember, I suppose.

Can you remember his son? He was crazy. Was his only son. Could never say a proper word – just murmured, grunted like an animal. Someone once split open his head with a piece of slate. They were immoral in those days. Children hated him. Hated Mao. I suppose the nickname was appropriate.

Do you think that old man at our shrine has been in the Army? It's the volume of his voice. His scars.

Have you eaten? That's how people say hallo, didn't they? Villagers, I mean. I remember.

You say he just came from the evening?

He was *bleeding*.

He is the only man alive who can do what?

Don't the Gurkhas want him? Oh, yes. They've gone, haven't they? But he is still illegal. Like Snakes. You gave him what? An old Identity Card.

But who is he?

No. Who is he really?

Silence. No movement. No more nods of the familiar head or the tug of a finger. She was dreaming now. May let go her arms which had been worn mother-like around her. She pulled at the blankets. And remained wide-eyed in the darkness.

So much secret. Hidden among the music of cicadas. Swallowed at evening by the depth of a cuckoo. The universe unyielding. No sleep.

In the darkness. Long after the boy – his other, less regular visitor had gone back to the city, who had brought him food fresh from the quickened city, kept his identify a secret. Together with the voiceless girl hiding him. Having sympathy for him, adopting him like a merged shadow.

Now murals breaking around him there will be no sleep. A habit. A caution of age. He knows always around this time someone is out there. Slipping through the marshes.

"Ay, day you speak nay of men. Yet night you tell of ghost!"

"Come out now!"
Just echoes cruising crazily into empty space.

FIRE HAND-LIT BY GHOST

THE GREAT JOURNEY OF EMOTION first entered the deserts of Western China in 1965. Time of the unknown. Millions of reluctant settlers were ordered west – exiled, so to speak. Gansu, Qinghai, Xinjiang, suddenly found themselves on the progressive map of central planners. None of them were to ever return. Industrialisation, military, institutions, transport, all entered regions which had for hundreds of years been unknown. Areas of wasteland and beyond. No man's land. Such was the intention of military strategists acting under the interest of national security known as The Third Front, or San Xian.

Railways explored beyond the wall. Old myths were broken. From the city of Lanzhou into the oasis of Hami the journey was three days. Non-stop. North-west along the fringes of sand and ruins through to Urumqi, where an old Han necropolis has for thousands of years remained rainless. Korla, Kuqa, Aksu, Kashgar and Soviet Central Asia. The Great Beyond. The historic journeys which had entered, the railways which now enter and go further beyond, which are said to head into nowhere. Spearing deep into the southern reaches of the Tarim Basin then disappearing. Such strange traces of less ancient man. There is nothing mentioned of them in books or guides. Illusive, snake-like, more private desert routes. Origins secret. Maps and charts have never given precise identity of their inherently three dimensional existence.

Passenger trains hardly stop once among the dry land. All trains had a capacity of water which lasted one hundred and fifty miles. Travel was almost always overnight. During which the outside temperature fell sharply. Geography condensed. Darkness. Sleep was one alternative. The ghost of a landscape slipping from window to window. During such hours of whistling remoteness there is only a window. The darkened velocity which said nothing. Simply the stars dying in the distance. The legend of forty great cities buried deep in the desert heart.

A travelling expatriate opens himself in near darkness. A hand somewhere. Gliding its way past his neck like the caress of a cat. There are no words. A ghost. A tango of white. He catches only the slide of movements. Visibility split into several momentary bursts over a hanging bed or splashed from uncertainty into a sanctioned room. A reappearance somewhere. Sprays of white incandescent against the darkness. Thrown forward then falling into a solid. A familiarity of hunch and twist through which choreographed a flutter of brass. He turns his head. The contours now in and out of the blink of light. A dove in mid air. More flutter of notes. Then there is no movement. No white lady. He cannot detect the movements anymore except for the warmth of the sheets which a sleeping body had left only a moment ago. An alchemized spirit. Change of mood the way darkness transcended light.

Who was she? For a moment out of sleep. Then he remembers. Those many communicative months. Yes. He knows about the feline slide that is upon his forehead now. Recognizes the speed with which this hand withdraws the morning curtains. Modular hands, fingers that adopted like eiderdown to every touch. Nothing else but her hand of words. Her white back. Her hair a river of darkness against the window of climbing dawn. He adjusts himself against the frame. He can see the silver blade in her mythical hands. An apple. Then whatever she was doing stops. She retrieves back toward the suspended bed then hands him the apple separated in two. White in the mist of light. He takes it. Looks up at her. And for a while he thought there were tears in her eye. But he was not sure. Always the light of dawn. The curtain of emotion.

He checks his wrist watch. Soon the entire carriage will be awake. The train heading eastward toward the old twentieth century capital. It was June 3rd. 1989.

The man returns again through the drizzle of evening light. In the minibus locals know as Fourteen Spaces which is like a travelling bedroom because it always moves into places of privacy. The unknown and often deserted territories of Hong Kong. He checks his wristwatch. 6:06 p.m. He watches each passenger slip off one by one. A casual shout at the driver before the next stop. Groceries, squawking chickens, old faces fading within scrawls of dust. The thud of a metal door. Then, he realises again he is the only passenger.

He alights about a quarter of a mile before the village. Standing in the solitude of light. He carries only an umbrella. Carries only the food fresh from a stall which he has brought specially for an old man. He starts walking. Softly emerging within the cocoon of trees. A fossilized school. No birds. No sign of teachers or pupils.

You and I, he said. We were among the courtesy of wind. Fire blizzard near darkness. Remember? I was still in school shirt and pants. And you, you were always in a dress of expressionist blue.

We were pushing each other over the imaginary cliff. Swinging. In a choir of branches.

We had no names. Only a forest.

Were we in love? She smiled.

Didn't you know?

Why did you not say?

There is silence. Until suddenly the pounce of a cuckoo.

You never even said goodbye, she said. Her eyes on the earth.

Are you sure?

Yes. I would have remembered.

A saunter of silence now. Her eyes glued momentarily to his. Are you sure?

They had met by chance again through the mute girl. The secret audience. Among the whimper of leaves skipping around them. Their childhood in the school of a forest surround where there are clatters of bamboo and bored branches that groan upon silence. Being watched, blessed, haunted always by the forest deity. Taai Wong. Sat as a throne of concrete once upheld from the firework of Mangroves. Listening. Can you hear? Throwing paper planes of memory backward and forward like bait on a fishing line.

Locusts were brimming in the hills. Prawns within the clear free traverse of streams and rock pools. Not in the classroom but through the windows. The mind always somewhere else.

Who ever knew we were here? Filling a room in equal movements. Equal uncare. We never wanted to leave this pendulum of extra senses. A thrill or a relapse – a timing, being held from gravity. Our faces in light of the terminus of wind. You. Forever falling.

Yes. And so were you.

Yes. Face to face we were falling. Knees to face. Your breath in my breath. Taking turns to send the spirit away.

Yes. You remember me, don't you?

The swing that was hooked to the oldest Cerbera. So old like an elephant's leg. Near the recent footprints of blood and always near the sacredness of a god. They had unified there when children. Discovered something they both loved: the pretence of flight. It was the perfect co-ordination. Standing in mid air face to face. He knelt. She knelt. Then he knelt again. Each time thrusting her backwards, each time thrusting him backwards with the uncertainty of darkness behind them. A haunt of bamboos somewhere forever clattering slow and soulless. Near a ghostly entrance – but when you pushed like that, into another ephemeral voyage, you no longer cared.

Like the actions of a seesaw but without the fulcrum. Without the divide or physical sanction. Togetherness. You were united. Breaking light. Breathing each other's erupting breath. Smelling one another during the dive as if acknowledging each other as equals. Both children. Both flying to paradise under a spell. But only a blizzard of wishes. Eyes then knees. Knees then back up upon the eyes.

I loved smelling the Yellow Orchid in you.

But you were heavier. Every time you knelt I shot back falling from another planet! My legs almost gave. So dangerous. I could have slipped off!

Within the whoosh of senses. Silence. They tell each other what they can remember. Then he would leave near the edge of light. Hitching the anonymous last ride.

Always there seemed a storm was approaching. Leaves curled and upturned. A forest sensuously swinging itself around and over an old school. A brushed encounter. Tentative wind. Oh... I can't believe it's you. His name was Kim. There was so much to ask in such a brief time. The sound of bamboos like the gathering waves of the ocean crashing ashore, covering embedded joy. A reconnaissance of things around the pinnacle of leaves smouldering before the playground previously brushed and burned by the old man. It can happen. A school reunion. He stood there before her in shirt and tie, collar undone and sleeves rolled up. A black file against the curl of bedraggled roots. His day over. She recognizes all this. The labels of city life from which she had derived. And here, the ephemeral isolation she chose instead. Counting back on tip toes. Only the detail of a dress perhaps. Her blue tint dress and his herd of lethargy. A play friend. Both in the sudden possibility of a passing figure, a patrol or a nonchalant dog, or the swing which was hooked heroically at the highest branch that was no longer available. Which they had dreamily dug up only because of their presence by the school, this playground, this mood within an introduction of stones which enhanced of them a series of playful manoeuvres. Being together.

You could almost touch the leaves. Yes. I loved it here near evening.

On your own?

No...

And, words, play, such wonderful seducers of people.

For a while behind plaster and leaves the small figure continued watching them, pretending to have previously left. Her silence blended of wind. A romance, she thinks. In between the school and the darkness and a god.

What is a menace? A creepy spy? Ghostly moves. She did not care. Her attitude of the wild. Not charming anyone. She knew of no boredom. Is constantly meddling. She will know what time of night to go spying for catfish or how one gets rid of dung beetles. Danger is somehow compromised because of her disability. She herself has lost count of the near misses. Night serpents lying across pathways like sticks. Only by treading directly over them will you know about them – but which by then was too late. From a habit of safety she always carried a cane. There have been many times where she entered and disturbed some vicious snake. Some breeds are red in the eyes and tongue. Killing it was easy. Good manners, someone once said. If it was not too large she would end its life with a fencing match. A natural instinct of play if you lived among hills and trees. Places they hid and temporarily lived. And in the New Territories, snakes, as far as she could remember, were often spoken of in two terms. One as the vile and poisonous, the kind her brood of cats fought against perhaps because of play. Common instincts, said LoudCracker. While the other was as illegal men, running across the night border. Ragged shadows or *Snakes*. How the term was coined she never found out. But whenever she hears them mentioned, the way whispers were phrased, it sounded more and more as if they were not human at all. *'I hear they'll be smuggling tonight..'* *'* – *two Snakes followed him through the woods.'* Because they only came at night, when there was lightning. Rain and screaming phantoms. Times where no humans would dare venture out. Not even her. In the wet woods belching of ambiguous movement.

Perhaps being invisible was good anyway. Because no one ever bothered you (only she against them) she was not required to leave for the city like they all did after the school's closure. Like her old friends May and Kim, whom both left even earlier. Who, as she will always see and know are people much like Master Wong, whose eyes never looked straight through you and never attain that voiceless back of a body. Supposedly it was like a flock of cranes landing. First there was nothing. Then they come one by one. Altogether and all at once.

Now and again in the brisk of light. It was some time before the arrival of May. There was only Kim, or Red Rain as she knew him had a routine of daily visits – if the city did not keep him. During which he brought food and news and precious company and often a toilet roll. At first she couldn't understand why he and the old man laughed and talked about it like confused children. She could find nothing hilarious. Till several days later by tugging at the old arm did he reply: We have no such paper over *there*. You only used thin bamboo sticks.

In his tie and shirt in her Choo Tong. He had found her in the old Ancestral Hall. Somewhere she felt one could continue play. Undisturbed in her private place only she knows, where she can go with the wind and nobody else beside the patrol of infrequent soldiers. Searching, always somewhere, in the grass or woods, the slide of illegal immigrants known as Snakes. There in the village shrine Kim found her, but at first seemed not to know her. His face and expression against the bedraggled ceiling. In an interminable trance, his body so still, frozen among the backdrop of collapsing façades. Broken spaces. A figure knelt in silence. Dusty knees. He could see she was chanting in front of the miniature Goddess of Mercy whom she had personally installed on the table. Now and then the song of laughing doves. It must have been June 25th. The birthday of GuanYin.

Remember me? He kept asking. Yes? The Herd Boy...

She remained half knelt. Between holiness and the past. But not alerted, not surprised. Somehow she was getting used to strangers. The transience of city folks.

There was not supposed to be anybody around anyway. The government was building no rubbish tip then. Nobody had ever returned since the last widow died. Perhaps the odd European tourist taking snaps of the Gun Tower, reputed to be one of the only two existing throughout Hong Kong. She has never understood why the tower fascinates. Why it was taller than the rest. Why there was always a churn of wings. The fortified doors. During daylight she would quickly skim pass fearing a white ghost might suddenly appear. Call her name or befriend her.

And there he was. What did he say?

Funn? Her name. Little Ah-Funn of silence? *Is* it you?

There is a shrub they call Fire Hand-lit By Ghost. The old man tells me in Cantonese that sometimes it is known as Ghost Lanterns. The term often used in books. A common shrub well known in South China. One tells me about its medical history. One tells me from experience of the fragility of its common name. So many nicknames! But I only see a bare shrub with no sign of flowers.

He has promised to take me there again in June. At the burnt mountain behind the terrace when there will be fiery blossoms. Like when we were small.

I don't know.

She drops the pen. Folds away her spectacles then blows out the candle.

There was no wind. She sees him in her courtyard half naked.

"Good evening."

"Yes .... I didn't hear you come in."

"No. Surprise, you see."

She moves toward him feeling the fade of warmth. He was at the tap, his feet within orchestral waters.

"You always bathe here?"

"With your permission?"

"Only kidding."

"I would wash here every day if I could. City water is coarse. You probably know that by now."

"Yes."

"There's no sign of them. Where are they? Shall we look for them?"

He turns off the water. A huge silence. The ease of a forest. He dries himself under the ripples of light then puts on his white shirt. Rolling down his trouser legs. His bare feet stepping out of the shallow pool. They walk away together.

"Don't you need your shoes?" She points back.

And, as if terribly guilty, he swiftly retrieves them without even the formality of socks.

Early evenings. Songs of cicadas in their cushion of darkness. No twilight. No switches of light. They go through the ephemeral flotsam of red. A time when May wished to be alone. With the romance of mood, smell of ease, a release. It would be perfect here was it not for the impact of night and mosquitoes, and sometimes her voiceless friend nagging at her arm, wanting her safely indoors.

But now walking through flotsam of red. So swift, nothing ever waits. Where her attention was focused. Noises in the distance. A whine or a hum of a vehicle, she thinks. A last ride. Where Kim, this friend of the swing, was due. Time so precious as they once again enter the membrane of leaves.

"1974? 1973? It was one of those years."

"You left in the night."

"Yes. Sorry I stood you up. Forgive me?"

"Just kidding..." She smiles. Turning away her head into the shadow.

"When did you leave for England?"

'Well..." She looks away again. "A few months after you. I think."

"It was sudden. All so sudden, wasn't it? You into the arms of a queen. And I, into the arms of a war..."

He drifts from her toward the school gate.

"I could never have known where you were."

"No. There was never time. Nationalism and war. That replaced childhood. I fell back into my family of wrist watch dealers. Yup. That's right. 1973. We were selling time in Saigon. Another exploding city. The only big difference was the old French clock tower. Its first chime so dignified. While the half past - my favourite. Meaning home time. Fruits, imported goods, the city fumes. The place was easily warmed to."

"Then the invasion...."

"Sure. May 30th 1975: I was at the City Zoo at the time. Near a black panther."

"It must have been awful. How did you get out?"

"We flew. Flew years too late. Our order or living dismembered. There was nothing left. The clocks and Swiss watches and the great accuracy of time and moments we left behind. Time had run out on the city. Was no longer available. Here, see this watch. 1967.

"We were all nations. Hindu, Chinese, French, American and Vietnamese. Not simply the back waters or some faded civilisation. In my childhood there was the Great Temple of Shiva whose myriad of arms was said to wander at sacred hours. People were welcomed like Amritsar, whom some believed was the female Buddha and laid their offerings in accordance with wishes. But even they, their permanence was to leave us. You see, the priests knew it was time. The great golden doors closed on Thursday. A month before the street sat without a soul. Trash bins not full of trash but full of rifles and uniforms abandoned by National troops who themselves were abandoned by faith."

"*National* troops?"

"The soldiers against the Viet Cong. Against the invaders, who were no great knights in shining armour come to reclaim a nation. From manholes and underground grids they emerged covered in muck and crap. They did not look human. Not like the way they talk of it in history books, in a panegyric of statues. There was no one to greet them. No one, no traffic, nothing. There was a curfew and the entire city hid indoors for almost three days, hearing nothing more than rockets explode or the occasional scent of cordite. No one dared venture out. And why? All because of them. Invaders. A new regime. I was halfway between the reality of danger. Halfway between the cage of a black panther.

"Some people must be born by a habit of always slipping like a breeze through parents and gates and warnings and war. In the place of abandoned animals. Plumages and lawn. Any time I could have been blown to pieces or blown apart by flying shrapnel. Died alone. But I was not yet an adult. I was not just anywhere. Not anytime.

"I remember entering the half closed City Zoo. I entered among the animal silence, where I felt it to be the safest place in the world."

The school. A god. A forest swing. She knew nothing about him. A tissue of memory. Only the school and the swing were the touchstone to their identity. Swirl of red leaves. Red Rain. Him and her, both transients of this long ago village. Him and his half naked body like Sabu. A most beautiful body. Brown and smooth and moist. In a forest.

The playground had been nothing more than yellow earth where one could fall and can pick oneself up again unscathed. There were no handouts of books or paper, every item was privately bought. Apart from name seals, the air of fans, a sweet for tears, a teacher and his wife - nothing else was provided. There were only leaves. Whiffs of splintered shadow. Always a god in a forest, an uncle of mangroves and stones lovingly watched over them in their playground moves. But somehow for May she never joined that hand of games or skipped into fantasy. That was her character. At such times there was always a Mute infant waiting for her after school. Never smiling nor saying much. Like a sparrow at the window, sometimes and sometimes not. Like Kim. Both had an air of transience about them. May first noticed him not at school but after, when the gates were closed. Coming camouflaged by mud. Not ever looking at any one or thing as if a ragged prince. His mind with the yonder, his care of the senile herd trotting idly under a shawl of wind and leaves. A working youth. She had noticed them many evenings before with her silent friend behind private shadows. With her silent friend who loved nature. Who was a mystic of findings. Had a passion for moth pupae. They were collecting them when he suddenly passed. The lazy mood which she saw, the way they were coming home. Like an anonymous ink scroll she would see later in life. This holy friendship conjured through his appearance of harmony. She was absorbed by wishes of such an entrance. A jungle boy. Waiting for her near the circumference of darkness.

"I can hardly remember much. The wind in my ears. You almost pushing me off. No. You did push me off!"

Talking of themselves as children. Nameless. Only in pieces, in fragments of a shallow yet murky pool. Dreamlike. Without evidence or at times without witness except oneself. Like a smudged drawing. A tendency to find beauty in such accidents of ambiguity.

"It's so odd. Everything. I can't remember what we ever said to each other when we were playing. What did we talk about? What greeting or farewell? We never had names. Did we? A rendezvous by shadow and leaves. Not knowing how to ask for you if you weren't there. Nobody around. After school, after or maybe before sleep. But always immediately after dark. An area of posthumous cries where I could still smell the wild grass in you. By the rock pool. By a cooling herd. As if you never left that hill or ravine of Silver Birches. Any minute there was a feeling you may suddenly leave. Disappear and leave me alone."

They had walked through into another side of the forest. Out and away from darkness and found there a drifting stream. A bridge and a corroded cart. Languages spoken through collected dust.

"You do know where *he's* from?"

"The old fella, you mean?"

"Yes. The one whom you *two* seem to have given amnesty. Or was it simply that I am just seeing things?"

"You're not seeing things. And we're not amnesty."

"No." Her eyes spying at him from one angle of her face as she always does when she thinks someone is lying. "But I guess it doesn't matter now. Not in a few years' time. I mean with the end of British rule."

" ...If he has that long." She looked up at him. As if surprised of his bluntness, seeing the darkness under his brow peering at the water's edge. Both of them leaning against the cold rail. There was this peculiar humour in relation to the old man. A strange relationship. That first time when they met she came across them by the Ancestral Hall where he was again barefooted, there had already been voices prior to their entrance. She was in fatigue from the sheer weight of groceries but her quiet friend insisted upon checking in on him.

Ahh leave me alone. It's been a long day.

No. You will like her. She is smart.

She heard them. Supposedly the old man was talking about her, she guessed. And the younger man had sensed a joke. Knowing people only return if there was money to be claimed. But now talking with Kim she knew it was all a part of their strange friendship struck up whenever he arrived from the burning city. From the daily commotion that is life into the solitude of this one man.

"Shouldn't we head back? Soon it will be too dark to see. Oh, I forgot you only date darkness!"

"I wonder what ever happened to my herd? They were a boy's best friend. My radar against dholes in the dark. The saddle home."

"You and Ah-Fun are so much alike. I wouldn't be far off if I said you were brother and sister. And the old man your uncle. Some great lost uncle, perhaps."

"Are you cold?"

"No. Why?"

He unfurls his jacket then slips it over her shoulders before she can utter a hint of refusal. Both his hands upon her slim shoulder edge as if guiding her somewhere.

She watched the darkness into which he had long vanished. From the isolation he returns to the city. To the voices and the crowd. She knows he has far to travel.

Then she turns. Finds her speechless friend by the doorway. She is smiling.

YULIN, NORTH CHINA, SEPT 1987

He stands up ten yards away from where the camel has stood under the intense noon glare. Its neck turning simultaneously. Now and again moving a fraction or now and again only its inquisitive head peering from a rim of sand. As if curious of him. For a while he has stopped working. Standing up into the desert. Letting himself be surrounded by a Green Wall and in distance by the outline of a Great Wall. The new and the old. But he is only interested in things living and growing. The difference between artificial and edible.

He pulls up his wrist and looks at the time. Two thirty. A frontier of greenery stretching before him. *Hedysarum, Caragana microphylla, Astralagus*, a horticultural shelter belt which holds back the desert like a river dam. Desert defences. The line of acacia and larch and willow rolling further inland toward the city of Yulin. Civilisation protected by nature from the encroachment of wind and sand. Or sometimes man-made nature. Artificial shrubs. *Latex legume* or Smart Plants. What he has planted during these weeks of work among the Green Wall.

Now collecting the implements he has taken with him, packing up the trellis and spear-like tappers which people find so fascinating in this desert country, he acknowledges the fact of the work was still *experimental*. A trial. Arboriculure by training but occasionally cajoled by horticulture. His contribution here was nothing major. No scientific breakthrough. The Green Wall which halted the invading desert. He was there to simply add a few touches. The 'paint work' of the project. Because the outer wall had been in gradual attack by goats which primarily are one of many causes of desertification. Once the skin tissue of vegetation disappears whether due to mis-management or the excess of activity sand will come abetted by wind. This eventually will lead toward the appearance of a desert-like state. Uninhabitable to life. Planting drought-resistant trees has proven useful, but requires analysis and in-depth planning. Irrational planting will again lead to disaster. Uncommon in a country where *experimental* endeavour seems notoriously pervasive.

Forty two *Latex legumes*. What he had brought from dawn from the Rodale Institute. Flown with them all the way from California and down into this remote Chinese corner. The camel endlessly pulling faces during the unloading of his cargo. The latex having a smell which the beast loathed. But was part of its special property which repelled herbivores who are supposed to find its man-made taste deadly bitter. A latex of 'bad flavour'. So far, there are more than eight hundred Latex bushes fringed around the Green Walls outer defence. All his months of solitary labour. His days near the desert. After which daily monitoring will determine the effectiveness of planting and rooting characteristics among the real legumes. But anyway, that would be somebody else's work. He yanks the beast, and begins leading it back to the city.

What appeared in the evening sky like a dark brood of clouds soon manifested itself as flying insects. A locust swarm. On the second evening they appeared. At first like a blanket, a sheet of swirling opaque. Then a plague. Capable of mass historical destruction.

Among the natives he was the only one with binoculars. It was like rain in a storm but without the thunder. Heaven's hunger. There was no indication of the size of this swarm. Only that it had already obliterated the yields of four counties. Wheat, maize, millet. Nothing could stop them. No chemicals were available. No way of combatting them. Called in on the scene were just three strangers who happened to be nearby the Environmental Corps. None of them specialists in this field of hazard.

He kept looking at his watch. The low sky. Gauzes of motion. Whose idea was this anyway? Mad. But it was working. Three hectares of cropland had altered colour. A menacing stir. A coolness he could feel against the burning heat. Through his binoculars he saw it all. Water exploding from within the fields. Fountains and sprinklers raised like lances in the air. Eruptions everywhere. Crackling life of thirty two diesel pumps borrowed from every corner of town. A rare rainbow envelopes them all. By seven thirty p.m. the desert air was floating about in sheets of moisture. It was a miraculous scenario. One by one the plaque raining down on them like pellets.

"Cut!"

And suddenly among all this was the word. This magician's word. A camera, a dolly, a story. An old film-maker. Kim finds himself staring at them. For him this was becoming a familiar scenario. Western film crews were everywhere these days. But this was the first rare occasion where he had seen one being led by such an old man. Eighty nine years. Sitting comfortably as strands of silver that were his scalp merged colourlessly against moulds of dried wood. The stone stillness with which he controlled.

They were already there even before he arrived. The western starkness among the locals who converge only to stare. Alien curiosities. A Big Nose. The White Ghost. What were they doing? And he had explained. "This is what they called *'documentary'*."

Something *personal*. A film of desire. But now he is leaving all this. There was something else to be done. Swiftly moving south and waving at the man sat in the desert sedan.

Thinking to himself. What a bad waste of water.

When he arrived at the river's edge everything was blue. There was a boy who guided him there. A boy barefooted whose thin signpost-like body in the bare landscape reminded him of someone. They are in the murmur of water. The rumbling of diesel pumps fading into memory. His feet sinking down on silt.

Like a resting creature. The SHP, or small hydro power station, lay sprawled like a dark tadpole. A tributary of the yellow river which has denied it life. Idle now. Yet nothing is ever useless in his thinking. He begins the inspection at the low diversion dam which channels water from the main source, finding it heavily silted. The forebay, the penstock (pipe), water entrances to the power house all undoubtedly needed preparation to lift it away from its years of neglect. What was a UN project. The boy like a wagging puppy following him to each organ of this umbilical machine. Moving with demeanour over and sliding down the penstock or encasing himself comfortably within a corner of the hut-like power house. Perhaps this is his playground, Kim thinks. Derelict machines have always been places of magic for children. Like distant satellites. The boy now watched him on the stone bank unfurling a folded spade, the one he always carries because digging and planting have somehow become his trademark in a country of agriculture. The small agile figure skips down with him into a narrow channel. Using his hands and feet to throw out the dry silt. Fascinated by Kim's folded contraption. Darkness crawling fast over them. Soon he is at the forebay which is like a square bathing tub sunk into the ground. He clears the forebay by opening its gate. Twigs, pebbles, rusted keys. The sky twinkling with stars.

There is no more light as he once again enters the idle power house. Noise of the invisible river muffled. Under the low roof he struck a match. Its nervous flicker throwing up the shape of a turbine housing. *Turbine unit capacity. 8000 kW.* The heart which generated hydro electricity. Then he strikes another match, holding it higher above himself. This time throwing up the image of a sleeping boy in the stone darkness. Tired probably after the day's play. He must have slipped away behind him. Curled away in the corner of this small world he seems to so love. Now fast asleep. *Everything in this country is fast asleep.* He lights the old paraffin lamp. He lifts off the lid. Whatever was wrong would be contained in here. But he is very still now. Unmoved. A black well which spilled up the murmurs of a river.

When the boy awoke there was thunder below. The hollow ground shaking. Dusts of the wooden roof scattered over his bare arms. It was a shock. He could see nothing. He runs out into the darkness and plunges into a dark body. Feeling himself being firmly gripped.

"It's alright - only the *River.*"

The boy rubbing his eyes as Kim releases him then hands him something like straws and twigs. Like a rough bowl. It is a bird's nest.

Moonlight and transmission poles. This was what they followed on their way back toward the small yellow ridge they had left four hours ago, left an old man photographing *his* film. Running the dark landscape with the boy over his back like a sack. "Have to tell them about the power-" Knowing two days' preparation will be wasted if he does not hurry. Wondering if the fire was not already being lit and filmed and watched by half the town's population. *("This country has an historical habit of lobbing people at great problems!")*

There was the singing of birds. In the dark distance there had appeared a white light. A rising glow. It was now drawing up their tired inspiration and enticing them into its brilliant path like insects.

It looked like the sun was coming out.

As they approached there were fires. A line of burning. Then a second area of fire, then a third - under this distant circular of light. They could feel the warmth four hundred yards off. Could smell the fuel which had been poured to aid the flames. Closer and closer. The lick of flames raised higher as if turned up like a volume. And perhaps if they knew what burnt insects would smell like, can see the burning swarm plunged forward with flight - attracted by this artificial warmth and imitated light which as they came up close was actually an amalgamation of hundreds of light bulbs, each taken or borrowed from a silk factory or a public space or the train station – now powered and lit by the SHP electricity they had revived this evening at the river where youth can find their solace of play. Reincarnate spaces. They may sometime in the future recall the way the plague fell like incandescent flowers from the glory of their fake light and the rows of fire. Figures adding more paraffin. Burning away the darkness around them.

Kim moves in between fire and light. In the warmth of motional darkness. The old documentarist nowhere to be seen. His camera and dolly operators gone. There was a phalanx shouting indecipherable words through the deafening roar. Crackling through the night's depthlessness.

"Where are those film-makers? The white man, I mean."

"What?"

"The Foreign Devils – where are they?"

"Ah – you mean those Ghosts who lit the fire-"

Yes.

After the first many weeks May had almost forgotten about the old man at the shrine. Forgotten the sinister way in which he appeared from beyond. Forgotten his casualness toward brutality and the relentless warnings of unsafe structures. Asked him less and less as he relegated himself more and more within the texture of the ruins. During the last part of April the rain and the isolation were ceaseless. Lightning now and again thrown through the dark interior. Sometimes without a sound, no aftermath, only the whip of a glimmer seizing her gaze previously instilled upon a page in her candle spray of light. A white light which could suddenly enter and alter the mood of a room. Enter her thoughts. Water and light. As if the hills behind them were eroding and collapsing. In blasts of rain, shafts of thunder, looking up in a moment of deluge. Wondering. Was the world somehow being washed away and she sat, knowing nothing? No cares. They kept fires going all the time whether it was the butane cooker or the engine warmth of an earthenware or the obedience of a candlelight. This way they delayed the damp temporarily.

Can you hear the worms crying in the night?

During the night rain they would go through the carnival of croaking and under slide of archways and drips of glitter and find him still there with his fire and religion and folklore. His hat. His figure in and out of darkness from the lightning. Talking loudly, at times not even perturbed by a sudden bleach of light. And there she had realised for the first time how empty and open the shrine really was, like a small gymnasium. It would have, at one time or another, have been filled with huge vases and gilded incense holders – not his voice, his uncare of identity still a river of things telling them this is the room where the spirit of a person ascends when they surpass the age of seventy years. And he was seventy. At a place of past and present. Drifted into being. At the right space and the right time. Ready to go. His purpose in life over. Almost sleeping.

Fractured images. She was among them. Inhaling them. A childlife. A silent friend and a stranger she does not trust. An old man. But that was her character. Cautious. Never flung herself carelessly to people. Kept a private bubble. Chose her friends as carefully as taking the ace out of a pack of cards. Always moving with poise among crowds, conscious of her schoolgirl appearance which she feels one has yet to discard. Even when she is with Kim, in his safe bed of memories, she would move in the confines of manner. Grace, reserve, control, if she ever forgot such notions she was surely to lose herself. Yet at times there was a naïveté which overcame her caution. Certain faces like her quiet friend or Kim. She had suspected he knew the old man quite well. Probably more than he admits. There were so many names here but no real names.

"There are no conifers," said Kim. "In Hong Kong. There are conifers only in the New Territories. Hong Kong being subtropical maritime-monsoonal. Which does not explain the lack of palms."

"Nay," would add LoudCracker. "In early times folk only planted trees for fruit. People knew about remedies. Nobody knew medicine like now. That palm melon *there*."

"You mean the paw paw, uncle."

"Ay. Yes. It was harvested because of its 'tonic' quality. Nay the tropical image. And did you know during the Japanese invasion of Hong Kong there was a shortage of ginger? No?"

"Here." He goes searching among the holy table within the Ancestral Hall where Ah-Funn stored her own sacred findings. A table full of her special world. From feathers to quills, hornet's nest to lotus seeds.

She found it flowering the other day. Shell ginger.

"And by the way, amoy. Did you know the White Jade Orchid Tree you often pick flowers from is truly good in cases of bronchitis? Yes. Use the leaves, roots. Wonderful flowers. Fragrance with a use."

He was difficult to ignore. He was everywhere. She would often find him at morning near the school where she would hear the sound of leaves being brushed rhythmically like roasted shells across the moss green playground. Left and right with the broom as if rowing down a river. The creatures drifting around him. Cats squatted near him, cats cleaning themselves, cats receding like water. But they only accompany him when he is alone. Only within his presence would they wander. In his absence of reality.

And for a while May would simply watch him. Not letting him know her presence. Hoping he may reveal some hidden fact or manner they have yet to witness.

"The West knows nothing!" he would often declare. "We already knew the art of healing antineoplastic two thousand years ago."

"What?"

"He means cancer," added Kim.

And this was how these strange moments would sometimes go by. A period in her life where ambition was temporarily forgotten. And blurred memories held fast. Such things she would one day in her hurried future remember again and again and think miraculous. One talking of life and the other prescribing the herbs to sustain it. All of them individual. All of them with their own precise motives for being there. In the jittery colours among the ruins of loose chatter.

It was a time of herself. If ever her Mute friend was not around there was only herself. Or, perhaps sometimes there would be him. So really she is never totally alone. He would be somewhere, some place near and eager to talk which she no doubt did not want. But he was never intrusive. Invisibly mannered. A crash of chairs and he would be by her door. Never stepping in until invited. Asking if she was alright. Somehow she was beginning to feel parentally touched by him. That toothless smile which seemed to almost instantly render him a harmlessness. His avuncularism which was less authoritative, the kind which she had not been brought up on that is tagged by bad explanation and most of all wit. "Don't touch that!" In reference to a frog. *"Sticks to you like glue!"* Where beside the flurry of a Longan branch; *"Careful by that bark, amoy! There are Itch caterpillars – all over your body will be in rashes. Pah!"* He spits. Then mutters something incoherent.

She was beginning to get used to him.

During the fall of light if not accompanying Kim out on a bicycle the mute girl will be carrying the basket swinging through the ruins. The fall of ceramic tiles exploding beside her. She ignores them, ignores many doorless entrances like sockets with no eyes. Weeds and ferns rupture inside them. Now and again her slim body in an armour of shadow.

As always he has been walking about the fort again. Edged in and out of past lives and the presence of disintegration. Doors and windows which have left no traces, no wraith nor remains. Only pure earth in raw sienna at daylight and burning rapidly gold near the influence of dusk. This is what it's always like when he returns. Tired after the day's brushing. The lintel of the shrine – his chair. Pillars of granite for those who visit, for those who bring his food and tea and companionship.

As usual, he sat there like a pointless block of wood.

Eight now, he said again. Six, seven, eight. One less than the night before. Sad? Never be. In this world life is swift. Some will go and some will come. See that one's belly. Big is it not? You *will* be happy soon.

Ay... Could be an owl or that dhole who steals only at dusk. Over there is where it appears. That valley.

Her gaze followed his thick finger. Her eyes where the light is weakening, shedding a farewell, a tear. A clean space as he says. Where light is evanescent. Harnessing a beautiful series of touch.

LoudCracker lightly slaps her left chin now. A mosquito. It has drunk much blood. He reaches for his Socialist pocket and finds an incredibly small round metal container. He begins rubbing the Tiger Balm upon her brown chin. She, disliking the smell, pushed his arm away.

No. It's good stuff.

She places the flask of tea behind the entrance. The usual position where she will collect it again the next morning. She loves watching him eat, paddling in the rice and salted fish. Munching each mouthful slowly like a grazing cow but furious at the intake. The sound of a man who truly knows how to eat. A timing. Never a word, only the meal. The Iron Rice Bowl. Which is always quick and clean around the rim.

Soon he is collecting together twigs and leaves which earlier he had gathered near the school. He strikes the evening into red smoulder. The mute girl reclines upon him. Not sleeping tonight, he chuckled.

The fungi season better start soon. The dreams are very loud. I have seen the *them* again. Seen *him* among *them*. His Tang robes and goatee beard.....

As he talks, she loves the soothing vibration of his voice. The heart that promotes it, the warmth from his arm so much better than the fire. She never wants to leave his arm, hugging on tight, his spine arced like some Galapagos tortoise. Always there and never going too far. This two hundred year old creature which she found, her property, his existence only among her world. Her sphere she is now trying to create by drawing together two memoirs.

She will spy on them again. Alongside the school. The magma of cows. Through the filigree of smoke. In their forest once more near the missing swing and perhaps even in the bucolic presence of her guardian. That can happen, she thought. They will stay.

I will not sleep, he repeated as he always does near such a time. And sipped his tea like an elephant's trunk.

When her evening is not spent with LoudCracker and the unaffectionate cats, she may catch a glimpse of a departing figure on the road. Then blast down on her BMX. Surprising him.

Hallo, Ah-Funn, said Kim. Knowing it was her. Where were we last time?

She had been waiting for this. She liked escorting him out this way. Pushing her bicycle along. Going as far as the next village and waiting till he is finally picked up by the roving minibus to the city. Among quickening darkness and the observant border neons. He used to warn her like how LoudCracker warned her. But now he understands her.

Have you ever seen salt marshes? It's an old method by which people extract salt from the sea using a fine collection of stones. In the desert at Osondaji there are such stones. And long, long ago there was perhaps a sea. A shore. A city. What is now wind and desert. But the odd thing is the desert is like the sea. Shifting and covering and swallowing history and legends at night. The only difference is the desert never recedes like water. It has no law, no life. We call this invading phenomena *"Desertification."*

What was that? Do I love her?

Kim looks at her. Her expressionless face which reminded him of someone. Then places his hand over her head.

You can tell me that.

The mute girl was almost living with May now. She was the shadow of cautiousness which prohibited you from quiet zones dangerous to newcomers. What fruits are poisonous even when touched. Where not to sit, especially daywarmed areas which can cause serious rash of the glands. She messes things up. It is her habit. Unable to let alone objects. Like the broken television, the pendulum of the old clock, the granite which beats the rice under the stairs. She is constantly finding items of personal surprise to May. She finds a flute, she uncovers the white ribbon wrapped in a handkerchief. The one which they could identify in May's childhood photographs. Always there is her activity breaking the serene. Sometimes festering the city girl's impatience when she is writing.

She could cook where May could not. Cared for things in her quiet way. Her fluid pace. Her slalom of the huge room dimming more and more like a man-made cavern. Up the stairs on the crying floorboards or among the courtyard of decay. She is not scared. She has been before. In a time of barking echo.

May has never quite figured her out. A riddle. A starling singing within the branches that you can never see. Unpredictable. Formed from a corner and the edges of doorways. Always watching. A feline stare, unblinking. She was a being who befriended nature. A bird or a chick or a wet duckling tucked inside her blouse pocket. Or strange pupae found only at Autumn near the neck of a forest. She would suddenly show you this. Show you these gems casually overlooked like children easily overlooked her as a friend of trust. She was despised for her silence. No one came near her except to spit or push away her evil presence. The inauspicious thing. Conceived of a fox. The big sister she found under the arms of May.

There was the tap under the great mango. Tin shacks under alcove of leaves. Dogs barking. A boy with a wet nose. Colours of children skipping and jumping where sounds perambulate the course of evening. Some maybe running in fear from a haughty goose or the crawling poison of a centipede or a caterpillar – a boy with a wet nose may want to kill this but hesitant – pulling back – reticent until the approach of the wild girl whose casualness toward human fears may somehow have led to the ignorance of creatures' rights. Her own gift of law of exacerbation or welcome. Like how she found money just dozing among the herd. Finding old jars and defunct shrines and blue river gems. Finding lost old men. You can never tell what she may bring in during the transition of midnight.

She makes a U-turn from the tumbling light. Goes through the tall entrance and finds the mute girl knelt beside the huge earthenware as if the furnace of a locomotive was being stoked with more thicket fuel. Nothing speaks but steam. A clean sensation. May signs like a half woken child. Her long hair and clothes falling unconsciously around her. Shoulders bare in the thin darkness. Near darkness. Close to a courtyard tap again. Where as a child a woman bathed her body with soap and songs before the heaven was filled in the canvas of midnight.

"I didn't know what I would find by coming here," she said. "I had no expectation at all." Not to find her. Not the old man. Not Kim.

To wash near tumbling light. That was what he still loved. Each evening Kim may or may not return. When he is among her he is always at her courtyard tap. Reappeared from a whim or a splash.

Naked to the waist, throwing water over and under himself and over again through the darkness of his Asian hair. His feet bare-standing within the skin of water slowly revolving and syphoned away down into the nearby marshes. The only tap that is left working. The other was at the old Mango. At such moments the mute girl and the old man would seem planets away. Leaving between the two of them the isolation and the school and a series of streams where water touches no more only the memory of a Herd Boy could know.

She tells him about her Aunt. A lady with a sweet voice. She says it was *her* insistence that a girl should wear dresses near evening. Keep her English patronage – till one day she goes back to her parents – which was not long.

"I watched her cut up those gargantuan worms using the sharp edges of tins. Big as fingers. Ooh – it still makes me cringe! The yellow ducklings gobbling them up as if they had never seen food.

"Sometimes I follow her to the fields. Her bony shoulders. Incredible the way she balances water, vegetables and thickets. She was always working. She had been widowed a long time before I arrived. A fleeting visit.

"She was a small-vague-half visible fraction of my life. Like the way you are. But how important!"

At night when she sleeps, the mosquito net is a sphere around her incarcerated by an outer sphere of darkness. Her friend always seems to dream. Tossing now and again within a midnight shower or the torrent of noises that may suddenly arise. Sometimes she will hear footsteps wiping through the wet grass and think it an animal or a hunting owl. But she sees nothing. When moonlight draws the world in blue. Only a window of metal instead of glass. The cicada overture. Perhaps the occasional human shadow running from a nation. Sliding through lightning like water.

One morning after being awoken by a repeated thunder, she found her friend standing above her among the brightness. Her face red and excited and grasping a weapon. May suddenly realises the scenario. A dead Asp laying dead below her, at her feet, near her flip flops.

She has saved her life.

And so it is a time where everyone guards something. Whether a cluster of walls or a memory of deeds or the sensations of flying. Preserved silently, like film or the way Egyptians preserved their kings.

Ay, Yes! LoudCracker smiled. Did I not promise to tell you about *them*? And *Him*...

But the mute girl has no time to listen. Not tonight anyway. She leaves him food and a series of gestures. She has no time to watch him eat and grumble nor see the way those cats rotate around the bowl. There are so many things she must care for. She will return later.

You will be back?

Silence.

Perhaps he wanted to tell her something. A dream, a series of lies. Maybe almost everything. Sometimes he felt that way. His life in words, in amplification and in Japan before and after the war. How he escaped the evil years of the late sixties by smuggling himself into archaeology. Dark times. Nameless years. An incognito labourer. And later when times altered, after fallen names had resumed and power regained, only then did he emerge from hiding. Living in daylight. Voices again. Yes. He would like to talk about them. Time, places, order, always a part, an organ of civil service life. There were strange mythical ways of reading them. Never know what one may do next. You may have had a life of engineering but tomorrow you could be advising on economy. On foreign affairs. Or be sent to the wastelands of the west. In continents of war. No law. Where you took what you want or traded what you want. Drifting rivers. Drifting away the mind and spirit. Drifting away to forget whatever international law you may have just broken.

And now sitting comfortably within nothingness he knew he had played the game well. Flung away the curse of reason when it suited him. Left them behind. Left China. He pours himself more tea and glances at the table of offerings directly behind himself. Who can possibly know he was here? This place forgotten and abandoned. Who will ever find him?

Suddenly the cries of the forest fall away. Death silence. He turns his head and remains very still. Windless. He knows it. The familiarity of it. All noises stopped without warning like that night before it happened. The remedial surprise. So suddenly. So cool. As if *they* would come to him again.

The following day, the mute girl returns and finds him missing. Not a sign. Only his blanket, flask and bowl. At first she is startled. And spins through the school and forest desperately looking for him, if not crying a little. Shouting out for him like a bad reception of a radio.

But it was the Gun Tower. By the fallen tree near that emptiness she was to find him. Knelt beside a dead Longan stump, where he is picking away a series of brown fungi. His longing-now available. Lingchi. The cure of dreams.

He turns and sees her approach. She is a bit upset. She seems frightened, but not by the Gun Tower. Now as the ravens forever churn lazily above them she fears she may one day lose him. She is afraid. His plump body and hat. Could one day disappear. Like a dream.

DREAMS OF LANGURS

LOUDCRACKER IS STANDING at the entrance of a blue desert. A thorium desert. Dunes rippling on the horizon, spitting dust, soon to erase itself. Like a holy sacrifice.

Next to him is a robed man. Very old. About two thousand years, he said. Before the existence of Persian Carpets. His silver tress pressed into a knot, slightly off centred. But not him. His eyes still sharp as a needle. Beard poised like steel dagger.

One moment a jungle. An interment of sandstones.

Suddenly a desert.

He is waving goodbye. They are departing. One is heading west with the sun. While the other is going east. Away from light.

How did they get here?

It was only yesterday they were confined among decorated walls within a jungle. Only yesterday. It was like being carried by an ancient river. A power storm which carved majestically through perilous jungle dangers. And now they are in the desert. Saying goodbye.

He looks back once and sees him moving away like a ghost.

He remembers. Yes.

First there was a dream. Always there is the dream.

One night under Asian stars blossoming and dying, behind sensuous walls, the man nicknamed LoudCracker dreamed. Illuminated dust falling in on itself. An extraordinary dream. Such epic proliferation and not quite himself. In and out the forest blasted unsettling showers of religious light. The barks dwarfed him, heaven high leaves engulfed him. Bewitching all sense of direction. Neither compass nor chiaroscuro of daylight gave him clues. But he moved through all the same.

And as it happens, other forms moved more rapidly than he. Hovering him from behind came hairy fingers. A river of hairy impressions. Came the hoard of Langurs among the wilderness of emerald, which he knew was no illusion, no prose of mistaken identity. Such escort at the midnight hour. One Langur may smudge him with great pride. An army of Langurs will award him royal insignia. For even a forest which once cried no life now seemed safe. And he was their leader, appointed by obeisance. And when people saw this, they ran home to tell things miraculous.

The sandstone wall remained frozen cold even though there was sunlight from the tiny porthole. Which was his only view of the outerworld. His face almost interminably against it. Hands chained. Facing a wall and a sorcerer's jungle. They took him there by darkness. Arms of rifles and bodies of grenades. His kidnappers. Now blindfolding him. Tied him sprawling like a bat in mid air. Whipped him. Caned him beneath his bare soles. The damp bareness. A prison in a jungle. Then they left suddenly. Swiftly. His flesh peeling. Leaving the door open as if danger or beast or a napalm was in approach. In sudden alert motion like a herd of deer slipping away from the hunt of a lion. Leaving him vulnerable from behind. Still chained. Left him within a cubicle of art where faces and legs strut from walls in frozen ecstasy. As if beauty wanted to touch his old body.

You're making a big mistake! I am no mercenary....

You're lying!

The stench of urine more apparent at night. Blood stains and remains of previous occupants. Traces in the dark. Forever explosions and flashes in the distance. When the jungle seems dead. He could see only one way. The liquid motion within the figs and vines. Nothing but the wind brushing branches. The cloth of bats dispersing and recollecting among the stars like sand falling into place. Only the moonlight lets him see, now. His view nothing more than a egg-shape hole which fits well to his plump face. A draft. A vulnerability. A reiterating fear of the unknown. Feeling himself at any moment the prey of some jungle predator. He had seen corpses of war attract carnivores like dogs in a street. He could never himself imagine the web of war again. Caught within. At his age.

Imagination. At such moment in life. This can kill.

Sometimes after two or three nights, he might swerve as best he could and find behind himself a passing shadow. Abrupt creatures. Lusty jaws near the corner of one's life. His soul. A clouded leopard, a wart hog sometimes, or the occasional rare bluster of Tregopan Pheasants. He never saw the same creature twice. Never saw his captors again. Only footsteps along a corridor. By fours and twos, even singly. An extremely long corridor, he is certain. He has heard his own shouts echo. A longitudinal abyss. There was only him. And the wonderful nymphs dancing for him upon the ruined walls. A dance of time. Long ago when there were elephants in decor. Chariots, slaves, craftsmen, silk and saffron in their thousands and thousands. Thousands of men. A king. A shattered relic. This man who came to steal its remains of power. Now, feeling the awesome might of a dead empire. The moist jungle. In the pilferages of war.

He runs his fingers along the dismembered torsos and bits of something's tail. Suddenly he hears laughter. Out of this cubicle of influenza, out of screams he could hear joyous laughter. Skips of merriment. Voices immune to jungle dangers. Gravitated him. He notched up his head and looked through the porthole and saw them dancing not far away in and out of a turbulent rope. Girls loudly sprinkled. And boys, some pushing, others fouled the rhythm. And swiftly, their momentum would be gathered up again.

He observes the evening light spraying them like a pool of dust. They are singing among the abstract mangroves. He tries listening in. Hearing only the music of bombers whistling above him. Somewhere. Another time.

When he sleeps, pressed and hanging into the wall, among the tearing pain, he hears Mridanga drums. Beats of multiple explosions. Flickers like a dying projector. He is not sure whether illusion or death. Perhaps a defoliant of pain. Whirling around, chants and cymbals in esoteric coquetry. Mostly his sweat rolling down his brow like a perennial stream. And the breeze of bells and tinklets may occasionally lap him. Release him. And so he sleeps. And dreams. And sees her again. Floating. Flying. Her ocean of silk billowing down the long corridor. He would want to call her. Halt her from flight.

Where are you all? The Immortal Empire?

He knew his echo would slip through branches and pinnacles as easily as a breeze. Alerting nothing. He often dreamt of the women of another world. A white angel. A watery nymph. The kiss of life. But silence. There is always the jungle around him. Mocking and telling of no escape.

> *Ay up in those leaves I hear*
> *Explosions tumbling like air*
> *In a thousand dreams as in a*
> *thousand stars as in a thousand*
> *eyes – Where?*
> *Is that a Tang voice I hear?*

Some whispered by him. Others not. Sound and voices seemed omnidirectional. Rhythms everywhere. And for days he ignored the voice of insanity calling his. He must not answer. He must not give in.

Who are you? Is that a Tang voice I hear?

No. Can't answer, he tells himself. Mental restraint. It's just the jungle, he told himself.

Always he would say, if I ever get out, I'll have to quit. I am getting too old. But never knew his particular skill was always being planned within the near future for some other equally perilous nature.

Perhaps he will go and see Akino. At least forty years now. She was so wonderful the day he left her sculptured among the garden. Mata ne, she always said.

No. Ridiculous. How can he see her? He nearly bloody killed her. Not a word. He just disappeared. Not a letter. Vanishing like that.

But he had to leave.

> *The wind so fresh, the sky so high*
> *Awakes the gibbon's wailing cry*

She used to think he liked such poems. Our happiness. Her silly tears. Sometimes he thinks she was taught to cry, always silently.

Rubbing the wart on his knuckle and telling him *things will get better. You'll see.* Which was always a soft, comforting lie. Etched in her faith. Her culture. He's always hoped afterwards, after she recovered, she has married somebody else better. Her own kind, perhaps. Someone with an identity. That paper stating what you are. What you can do and not. Whether or not you have a future.

He left because there was no future. Not in the service of Japan. Ainu, Burakamin, Okinawans, Koreans – these lists of non identity. The silent dispossessed. They are Japan's faceless crowd, unaccepted as nationals and unable to leave. Not like him. Searching across the sea till he found a granted shadow. A safety device like part of his organ. His ancestors who crossed deserts on strange grunting beasts and sold in cities where they thought of nothing but silk. Till their schooners on sand adapted into trails on sea to follow the spine of land. Seeking a land to offer them shadow. Simultaneously blended among architecture of another space. Another race.

A torrent whistle. A sudden thunder breaks his thought, now. He looks through the porthole.

Is that a Tang voice I hear?

An old man is alone among beautiful gestures of dance. He is giving in. Near death. Giving into dream. Feeling memory torn and falling from his white arms. In a hall of dance he decides at last to answer, to hear the predestine of death.

"Far, far away!" he cried loudly. "I come from far, far away. Who the hell are you?" The corridor shuddered. And silence. Silence of the singing jungle.

How far exactly? What period? Can you hear?

He stood up. The chains rattled. Where is it coming from? "You tell me first."

I can't remember.

Long, long time ago. So long. I've lost count and idea.

"Don't talk dung! What caterwauling good is it if you can't remember?"

Don't know. What good am I?

"Speak up, you sound like some bad echo!"

Echo? You're right. You don't expect an echo centuries old to be
able to speak up. Do you? Who will listen?

"Shout harder. Somebody will."

That is true. But among this interment of emerald, even you know
there is only echo to catch a voice like the strike of a bird of prey.
And I have not spoken for so long, not to a fellow Tang man anyway.
If you pardon me, The Great Wall was not even collected when I
walked the land. Ay... Buddhism had never crossed the desert then...
Never even reached Samarkand.

And silence. Nothing. Only the jungle exchanging its cries.
Dazzled by a merry-go-round of emerald butterflies.

"Well." He shook his chains. Sending noise out and along the
corridor he has never seen. Only felt. The fear. "I must be talking
to a ghost after all! Hell. How can this matter now? What does
anything matter?" He suddenly knew his mind was with the jungle.
Lost upon its bed of chaos.

"What did you say you did while you were alive?"

No reply.

He is standing with his ears glued against the wall. Feeling he had
no arms. Smelling like the wall which he has become part of, his
body lost among them where there are fragments of dismembered
arms and heads and torment of animals like a badly arranged jigsaw.
He is listening in. He knows where the voice lives now. He
obediently listens. *Can you wait? Can you hear? Are you there?*

It does feel good talking now and again. After a thousand years.
Confucius! Has it been that long?

Some nights I hear explosions from the jungle. Smudged through
branches. A boy screams and nobody answers. Pain. Yes, I can
curb that. But what is the point?

Alas! Rewards of duty unspoken by lies enjoyed in the human
heart. I cannot fathom the exact leaf to leaf misconduct. Wait. Ay, I
don't think common law was given... Such a long time, now. My
jaws are hurting already. I must remind you this *was* long long ago.

Somehow men who claim to lead also claim omniscience in every
profession. But refuse advice themselves.

Upon my cordial departure from prime minister Cao Cao's
itinerary service, he summoned me once more, drawing all my
attention in diagnosing a chronic headache. Yes. Diagnose.

Yes. I used to heal. But rather prefer preventing the problem first. Always I advise people, always tell them about therapeutic exercises. Aping about is fun. All of us were once cosmic systems. We are flesh and blood. A travelling jug of liquids. You must wriggle like a bear – occasionally as if a raucous monkey. All such fools gymnastic aid the physical body and promote the organic stream.

But they think they know better.

Anyway, I remember telling him it was no headache. I told him it was deadly serious. Told him I needed to operate. Open his skull – that was all. A simple removal of a tumour. Yes. The growth of antineoplastic. But he suddenly called me an assassin!

He had me put to death...

A death from the living, anyway. Such sweet rewards when I acted honestly under my profesa headache, then the land would have been a place of peace. There were miserable sion.

I was locked away for helping mankind. Speaking for life.

If only I told him it was simply wars in the Three Kingdoms Period. If only I told him it was a headache, it would have saved thousands of lives and altered the history books.

One practices art in a time of power. But after all, it was my sworn profession to heal. Truth was my downfall. In those feudal times people did not believe a man could be cut open and stitched back up again. Not the evil ruler Cao Cao, anyway.

There are medical journals which I wrote. *'Hua Tuo's Book on Acupuncture'*. My *'Faxian he Yanjui'* was lost during these isolated periods of eternal interment.

Anyhow, so much for human existence. Barred from the outside world for so long. You can only turn good at counting. Millimetres of light.

There have been travellers who have passed on wafers of time and believed who *I am*. They said they were going to release me. A silence forgotten among a dancer's land.

They wanted the key of knowledge. But I tell them, I don't want man to rescue me.

I don't need mankind anymore.

Don't want them to rescue me. Always they will want something out of me. Only the jungle now. And the faces of tyrant rulers cascaded and buried by figs. All dead, you see, from their own self festered wars.

You know, women used to grace these floors like transparent angels.

Hear that?

Another napalm. Someone is crying. Pain. Yes. I can curb that. But what is the point? Imprisoned. Condemned by mankind....

Ay, it can't be helped.

And so the evening comes. He is watching again the children in the distance. Singing a finale. And the voice of cure – his neighbour. Tired and asking for pardon. Sleep. A ghost who views no purpose. An immortal, perhaps?

The girl stared at him lovingly as if staring at the fire which would only last till midnight. He was like stone. Maybe sipping tea now and then to clear his throat. No light between them but the fire. A percussion of calls gradually surrounds them. He begins to mutter again.

After the explosion, after I had made my way here – I had almost forgotten about *him*. *Them*. Wounds of sleep. And now I can't close my eyes anymore. Restlessness. The only way in curbing the dreams and nightmares is what he told me. The cure of dreams.

From where I come there are escorts near death. One is white. One is dark. Figures of conical hats and abacus and bemused smiles which unexpectedly visit people and are known to have a terrible timing of humour. They say they can appear anytime and in any guise and manner they wish. One is darkness and one is white. Counsellors of death.

Yes.

I would be dead was it not for this man.

This legend.

He looks up into the fading yonder. And was suddenly back in the desert. Rambling its shoreline when he notices a scuttling in the rim of dunes.

A Langur.

He stops. It stops, like a reflection. Clowning his moves. He stares fondly at the creature. There is nothing else around them but sand and sky and light. A light that is brimming weakly. They remain that way for a very long time, just staring each other out till when finally the Langur appears, almost a silhouette butted against the line of fire.

Is that how they say goodbye? Waiting?

It was cold now. He must go. The desert night temperature falling like a guillotine. The Langur gone. He was no longer in safe hands. No safe guidance. A war wind comes over and wipes away his last sweat. Last drip. Just like the way that night the Langurs came, he was wet all over, when a whirling breeze slithered in through his porthole – his only view to the outside jungle.

Looking out deep into the jungle for the very last time.

Apart from leeches which suck your blood, larvae, which are like maggots that have teeth, eat right into you. Feeding on flesh and blood like a foetus. In the darkness and his own crap, he never could tell what insects were hanging off him. Never knowing what he had stepped over. The insect gymnasium.

Occasional talks with his neighbour, Hua Tuo, the legendary doctor – if that was who *he* was, mainly evolved around observations collected from his porthole, which describes nothing but wars since the Khmer kingdom was built and swiftly abandoned. The Hindu and Buddhist faiths, he said, were really a political weapon.

It's terrible, he continued. *It seems that through time people have mistaken the meaning of Tonic as something consumable regularly. Unconsulted. Only exercises can prolong life. You should still find this in my journal 'Frolics of Five Animals'. Not expensive tonic. Not aphrodisiac of rare life forms.*

By the way, they will soon be back to kill you. Are you afraid?

Don't worry – if you're still worried. My door has been opened hundreds of years and no beast has ever considered me tasty in any manner.

In the jungle it is only man that really concerns you.

It was full moon when it happened. The breeze slapped him and he slowly got up feeling blood returning at the arms. The moon's searchlight in a ballroom circles within his cubicle. There was only the usual midnight sonata, perhaps slightly faded and cushioned in a way. He saw the moon so close to him. Its family of stars blinking and dying thousands of light years from him. A place no one in the world could possibly find. Depending who you are.

Remember tonight ... Hua Tuo kept saying, while he licked at the drip of the wall. His lips against the stone lips.

Remember. Tonight, when the moon is full. And if you're fortunate, you might see the unicorn. Relative of the Vietnamese ox. But remember tonight .... You must look out into the night. Tonight!

All cries, all the world, suddenly crashed into a solid halt. Dead silent. Nothing.

That was how he recalled that night. Exceptional. Exempt of time. The stars above spilling down on him within the jungle where they skidded eliptically leaving tails of light like a comet. Accompanied by a song. The Great Doctor's chant. A meditation of lyric. As if the entire wilderness was listening. Was igniting up like an ocean of Christmas lights. Flickering wildly. Winking and shifting. In a circus of optical magic they pounced from pockets of darkness or descended with a sudden smash.

Coming from within.

There was no movement. Was supposed to be no life. He knew. The jungle silence awesome, but somehow like a pretext, an introduction or a theatrical entrance. He looks out again into a dream.

Saw the jungle was gone.

And moving between the nocturnal mist. *They.* Always careful. Like Trapeze Artists. The scuttle of stars. They were eyes, thousands and perhaps more strung upon the various nets of darkness. Yes. They were. There was a cavalry of Langurs. A powerful vision. Stepping only a second into the moonlight and into his startled view. Eyes of Cullinan sparkle. Scratching. Uncomfortable. Dreamable. In the power of her majesty. So silent. Letting the jungle speak for them. Cloak them around their silvery armour and the well of depthless faces. Like a communion of monks.

Letting you see them.

As they stormed through the jungle following the animal magic, he could scarcely recall how his tired hands slipped from the moistened wall. Fell from them as if his arms were severed. The reliefs crumbling. And so many unwanted echoes. In a corridor mostly marred by executional footsteps, not a river of silver.

But now, leading the way was the army of Langurs. Along passages of mangroves and fallen deodars and upon the backs of igneous boulders only they could know. Only their territory. Their easing of mist and their eminence as escorts. Sensing and knowing the safety over these accustomed pathways and improvised bridges initiated for human guests. A legendary doctor. An ageing smuggler. A need to be somewhere else.

He felt he could fear nothing. The fire power and sudden eruptions somewhere didn't matter. He was immune. They were among the moonlit hand of magic. Feeling immortal. Years from now, he will remember this feeling in the jungle. In the presence of a dream.

Hua Tuo, waving him on. Holding behind for him before they lose total sight of the rambling army. Their treads of light. Weaving and shielding their way against the treacherous jungle dangers. Never a sound. Always over sensitive triggers of death. A moist belly of *anti-personnel.* Always the tension of morning about to burst into the jungle. Any moment now, the new day's wash. Rinsing down on them with light. Carrying away their memoirs of internment and the guesses of a lost civilisation. How Hua Tuo sat in no hurry, no desperation to leave his cell, even after Halley's comet had crossed more than thirty voyages into the Solar System and scared the holiness of men.

I am so glad you could come with us.

His voice so streamlined.

It was informal of me. It has been a long time...

Always control. Like a balancing act. To gracefully emerge from his tomb of consciousness and be pouring himself into a palace of dancers. Rescued by a dream. Can that happen?

They had passed a courtyard orientating by the constellation, where golden leaves are buried and hidden and sacred, where LoudCracker knew well what they were worth. There were Langurs flooded around each crumbling step they took. You could feel their sheer power of presence. Sliding in-between their endless quilt of eyes and phosphorous and silver and ill respect to human antiquity. Parting like a Biblical wave in the ocean. Leaving. Urinating upon the pinnacle of broken heads. The face of gods. The hundred stone stare of dreams. The haunted kings that has caused him dreams now themselves facing rude faces of the night jungle. All nonplussed. Everything departing into a guise of emerald. Watched uneasily as the hillocks of faces of long gone tyrants stood pointlessly. Their wars ground and wind smashed into the sacred earth. As if the nymphs immortalised in stone were still waiting for them in paradise. Silhouette debris of birds exploding in the distance. All faded now.

In the desert they sat. The Langurs were a canyon of sand between them. Among the crest of dunes like thousands of tungsten springs. Still waving them on.
Come with us.

Drifting with the wind of radiation. Drifting with a casual ride. You have come to the crossroad of wind blown worlds. Nature and civilisation. How did you get here? There is an invitation. What are you saying?
He lets go the ounce of sand he had been holding. It falls away behind him. Instantly his hand senses a terrible rash. Yes. A poisonous sand. Nothing can live here. And the Langurs knew that. That's why they were moving on. Pulling up their wailing cries and soon sailing somewhere else.
He keeps glancing at Hua Tuo. Checking if the legend was still there and won't suddenly vanish like some optical fade. No transient nor a ghost. But remained miraculously solid as the morning aerosol sprayed slowly over the oblivious horizon.
A face of economy. Lean. Skin firmly hugging over the cliff-like cheeks of a legend. A landscape of frontal lobe diving over dim eyes. A shred of brow searching into the sands.
Have you been over there? He points, toward the oblivion. I think I came this way. When there was no desert. The city I passed must be buried now.
By this time the Langur army had disbanded. Remaining only a cluster. Picking, easing, flagging their tails. Till eventually all the Langurs had bid their farewells, casually, and gone home. Which must be as vague a notion as any. And as they depart, even years

after he had found his way back across hidden countries and tentative borders he will recall one's sense of well-being suddenly lost. As if an elder brother. As if the world will any moment be once again insecure. This majestic power in absence. Their concerto of cries that used up the world of echo.

They are leaving. Are you coming?

It must be morning. All is so bright. You know, I am not used to this kind of light.

They sat there. And left only near the fall of dusk.

THE SACRED SWING

IN THE MUTE GIRL'S light and the evening light and later the candlelight she writes.

Can this be real? When he leaves every evening he leaves me feeling this way. Was he real? Can you meet again – a faint memory? Destiny? To embrace a dream. Simply, idly, wishfully, swinging through the air. Someone with me. A boy. Holding slightly over my knuckles grasping heaven's rope. Someone who didn't like shoes but wore shoes only because he had come by promise. Someone who a child wanted to meet near the night window. As bodies light as feathers. We were taking off into the sky and up within a light and manoeuvre which nothing beside the power of love could stop. Falling into air. Falling off another planet.

Sneaked away near darkness. In blue, in secret. To be together. Footsteps dancing toward a forest. All around me the leaves are burning red cinema. Fire and darkness. A boy is waiting by a swing. He is in his best. I step on with him on that plank of air. We are so sudden. We met always immediately after dark.

There was a god somewhere, an uncle behind us who is stone who thwarted bandits and bad influence. A guardian near the depth of woods which frightened me. Unmoved. Watched over by holiness as we played. It was a sacred place. A Sacred Swing. After school. Immediately after dark. We move toward all this. Dreams of air. We would take off into the evening as only children knew how.

Kim turns as the cry bounces wistfully over him. There is scarce light. He is among all the swaying branches. The school path leading east smothered in red leaves, the blood prints barely visible now. He turns swiftly away, catches the playground of shapes near the corner of his eye like cool predators soon to react. Poised in time and space.

He comes from within all this after hearing the sound of a vehicle.

They appear from withered forms and shadow.

One moving faster than the other. A figure in the attempt of evading her shadow. Losing her identity.

He calls her.

She walks straight past him. Her eyes on the floor.

May! He calls again. But she hears him not. The mute girl shrugging her shoulders behind her. A crash somewhere, then the hush of several insects.

"May!"

She pushes herself from him to where there is the old well. Not wanting to stop or face him in her present state of mind.

"May. What's going on?"

He comes close to her. Hears her breathing out of control. But she moves from him again.

"What is it May? I am lost..."

"You never asked why I came here-"

"Neither did you about me. But what's that gotta do with it?"

She suddenly turns to him. Her face red and moist like water on white marble. He goes to reach for her.

"There's a man who loves me, Kim. He came all the way from Kuala Lumpur just to say he loves me. But, I am not sure. I mean – I like him. He's caring. He wants me – you see? I needed somewhere to think hard so I came here. Away from the crowd. This village in the back of my mind. Without disturbance. Nothing. What am I to do? Something has happened, Kim. Do you understand? Do you?

"Oh, I am too upset to talk."

She left him. Left a well of messages.

The rest of the night the house was only lit with two candles. The Mute sat awkwardly in front of cold food. Luncheon meat. Her favourite. But the city girl hardly quivered from her couched position. Wouldn't join her. The darkness around them switched deeper. It was the silence of motion. It must be that man. She could tell. The one they bumped into together at her city flat. A proper city man. *Where have you been? Leave me alone... Tell me what's wrong? I have nothing to say to you!* He was coming up the stairs as they were going down. The Mute rather enjoyed the temporary stay among May's three city friends. Most courteous as she fiddled through their rooms and the fake flowers and phials of perfume. But that man was insistent. Endless questions. *Leave me alone!* On the bus, the train, they finally lost him through the ladies and the rush hour crowd. And now May is silent. All caused, she is certain by that man. Who was he? Anyway, she knew May did not like him. Now that her own world was perfect. With the permanence of LoudCracker and the togetherness of May and Kim. All among ruins like the romance May spoke of from the book she cannot read. Cannot write. She knew nothing could change this.

Unmutual affections. She was never one for questioning. The label of insanity had been slapped on her the moment she entered the somnolent classroom. Under humid fans. The label of invisibility. Without a voice in society. A mysterious thing. Moving along like the wild night.

There were times when nobody could tolerate her. So she created her own world. Plucked foreign seeds and watered them. Granted them space. Privacy. And waited for the return of lovely colours. Like affection.

Nobody could understand her. There was no such policy. In a time and a presence when she found melons and gourds sitting neatly at the roadside in a cart or basket awaiting collection. She couldn't resist the strange affiliation and bad habit, she would commit sabotage. Play rugby with them. So the evening always ended in a collage of splattered melons and furious faces which converged noisily at her domain. She was chaos. If it was not a bundle of spring onions found pickled within the local lavatory it would be other properties mysteriously repositioned. Blasphemously executed near darkness. She was beyond law.

But now the scenario is always an elderly man seated and eating and drinking. A girl quietly watching. Her chin spying over her bare knees at the waves of creaturely colour. A world nurtured by her care. Occasionally a friend from the distant city whom she will follow like the way she used to follow Master Wong. Just the joy of accompanying a human voice.

Immediately after dark May headed in toward the forest and the school. Learning again how to hide. Perhaps retracing a route she often took long ago. She loved haunting things like the way her friend haunted this village. Chronologies and memories and order. A swift journey. She knew herself as the least patient of souls. Disliked bus stops, slow walkers and most of all the Hakka dialect – what her mother says in relation to her life, in relation to her future. A traditional girl by manner, though always her feelings have more or less guided her moves. The reason why she is here, within the slinky light, the dark school windows and the relative strangeness. All around her, the other valleys and streams and plots of land are changing, bulldozed and transformed into commercial and governmental use yet never here, not the school within a forest. Where each latter part of day she enters knowing that each tree will remain as they are and the school will still be locked up. But now her attention was suddenly caught. Something was different. A beginning. She panned toward it like obsession.

It was a swing.

She sat on it alone. A warm surface. Pushes back on tip toes. Throws herself forward. Her hair falling back swan-like. Being sucked backwards again. Her legs in the airy darkness like the togetherness of a pair of compass. A precision that was part of her gait. But she was no longer on earth now. She was free. Swinging through the holy atmosphere of the forest.

But one is never alone. Never wants to be alone.

He watched her from behind the old Cerbera. Waiting. Expecting her, years overdue. Was that an expression of a child? A smile? He could not be certain. She was a creature of flight now. Amorphous.

Up upon those final splinters of skylight then down again into the plunge of hungry shadows. At this moment in his eyes the most aerodynamic body in the world. The most lovely rendering of movement.

Leaves softly coming down over him. Darkness advanced. There was nothing to stop her. She didn't need to run from anything. Everything was up to her. She could do exactly as she pleased. The restriction of laws almost gone. And if he called her now, called her name, he would breach a promise. Intrude on her moment of beauty. And if - but she would never hear him anyhow. The rediscovery of a world earlier than that of a humid classroom.

He only approached her, made himself known as she fell back to earth. Her feet brushing the pool of leaves. His presence not disturbing but a comfort to her. She tried hiding her embarrassment. But was glad someone had been waiting for her. Two people in the right place.

He gestures for no movement.

No more words now. You don't have to explain anything...

They slowly embraced as only children knew how.

"It's for you, May."

"You rebuilt it?"

"Yes."

"Its nice. The rope is nice."

"Climbing rope. Are you cold?"

She breathes in the warmth of his body. Her feather-like movements finding comfort among his collar.

"You like the water don't you? I know. For you it's the sensation of cells and the negative energy. A traversed alchemy. Even in darkness you will know water. It seems always there. And soon it will be dark. Darker than what we were accustomed to as children. I've been in dark times. All of my childlife."

A cry suddenly bounces over them. She was about to speak.

"Don't tell me anything. Don't explain. Let me talk."

Did I ever tell you about the possibility of darkness invaded by light? Where midnight gradually became lighter. Brighter. In the desert there are nights like this. A falsity of emotions. Yes.

Speaking from experience – but that was something we would never want to witness it again. It's not natural.

A pause of words now. She looks at him.

We?

Perhaps he already loves someone else. She had thought about that. But she was in his arms. And she naïvely trusted this.

I have always dreamed about this place. To return. To stay here. And in the dream always there is lush pasture which awaits. Mist. Cows. Dogs falling in to greet me. I would be desperate to embrace them all. Jubilant. A desire to herd them toward something. A brook. A river. Some water near Silver Birches that is torrent and hypnotic. There I find myself gathering a fire. I am naked. Boy and earth. Promising myself I will never leave. Never. I retrieve movement from the whirl of water. The mother cow's groan would now seem distant. There is a fire of weeds and twigs. I start eating the prawns. In a dream in a place thousands of continents away. All my desire was to eat barbecued river prawns.

See this area of the tree? He touches the bark of the Cerbera. It's called the 'Bowl'. I have always known that. Always. But all the most important things in life I was to learn in the desert. The wastelands. The Great Beyond. Not in books. Books turn to ashes in the desert as if knowledge was forbidden there. I used to engineer environments, you see. Part of the Environmental Corps. Plant defences against the elements or implant decoys on cash crops to trap insects. It was like a child's game at times. Pulling nature by the leg. Fake this and that. Our aim nothing more than using common sense and the common mistaken sensitivity of God's creatures. A decoy of scent hanging off a pear branch can easily send mating insects haywire. To make the artificial more 'real'. Substitute them. Do away with chemicals. But in China, you can never guess what one may be doing next.

I learnt a great deal there. Not only the scientific value but about man on earth. For instance in some regions gesturing of generosity and good faith cannot be equalled as we know it. You should never share a fruit. Never cut fruits into two separate slices. People are symbolic. They consider such acts as divorced between two persons. A Goodbye in a way.

The direction of water seems to alter in the darkness. With a girl in his arms a man can only think of other times which are as wonderful as this. How sharing an apple cannot always comply with the meaning of generosity and good faith. Affection and affiliation in different cultures.

Where is she now?

I don't know. I didn't know her very long.

The rhythm of water's edge enters them. She had guessed he too was emotionally drifting. The reason why he comes back here. Constraint of affairs which seem to offer no other way out except to run at ephemeral moments like water.

Were you in love with her?

He was silent for a moment. She could hardly see his face.

In the desert I dreamt there were bluebells.

My only wish was to be among the ashes of books. But that was never a good policy. I am a person who knew well the meaning of guilt. Being haunted. And she was a soul who knew no guilt. No pity of yesterday. Life so casual, so indifferent against the laws of man. If in a street I accidentally knocked into someone – I would be the first to admit my fault, apologise out of manners. But she was not like that. The affairs of her geography were never considered as a matter of self responsibility.

Sometime ago by chance I met this very old man in the deserts of Gobi. An indescribable man. It turned out he was a film-maker. A veteran, who haunts the present because of the past when images were of a ravaged country torn by its worst ever civil war.

Somehow in early 1989 I met him again back in Lanzhou. Something *personal*, he said. A rendezvous, a farewell? I don't know. Anyway. Must have been sheer coincidence, I suppose – as they call it in the west. But in the east, it is known as "reincarnated souls".

Are you cold? Shall we head back?

A voice and a silhouette. A warm cuddle. Now, that was what he was to her in the darkness. What they will be like in complete darkness she does not yet know. With a forest behind them. Seems to be drifting over them. Carrying the blessings of a god which eased softly through the leaves. Nothing to disturb. A safe feeling they both discover, this child space where all things are said.

Kim, at least tell me what you did there ...

He rode out toward the darkness. He had missed the last ride and so borrowed the mute girl's BMX. Standing on a high wall May could still see the quivering dynamo dashing south. The only moving light there was.

REINCARNATED LIGHTS

GANSU PROVINCE, NEAR XINJIANG, FEB 1989

THERE WAS ALWAYS THE EVENING SMOG. The long chilled-out cry of the last desert express. Its distance. From the window of curtains there was the old city. Hinted of culture and religion. Not as old as the river which divides it, yet older than the darkening room from which this view was possible. During the late seventies there would have been endless documents here, maps and details of nuclear zones which may or may not exist somewhere out in the desert. There were then no windows. No evening light.

The Lanzhou Institute stood as a series of intermingling rooms of secrecy. A courtyard of scholars shifting backwards and forward. Desert, hazards, geological and arboriculture – to name a few of the academic stations. Sometimes a mystery to outsiders. Sometimes a mystery to themselves. Each institute operates indigenously. Some are just across the street. They do not seem to talk to one another. Always politely stroll past one another. Their days divided between the Great Beyond and the wall of privacy.

The Yellow River entering the merge of architectural patterns like a torn red dress. On polluted days it was said the water turned bright blue. In a room of windows they could see its glittery drift in limbo as if it represented everything of the city, half swallowed by shadows. Distant. Under the demure music this fragment momentarily clustered.

"Kim."

"Yes." Suddenly turning his attention from the light.

"Ask Professor Zhu about Osondaji. In relation to the "Howling Tomb" the locals spoke of there. Has it been identified? Has it been dated?"

They were around a table of delicacies. Three men, a woman with red hair. They are dipping bread into fourteen assorted sauces. The music is awful.

"We break off the rail at Hami. The army will fly us over Lop Nur. A two hour flight. Then hit the road at Ikanjubmal. From there we will need supplies – a guide, transport, a translator who can speak Uighur. There are just three towns along that thousand and twenty three mile journey."

Mostly he would refer the information in English. Sometimes stutters of French.

"It looks like we are only allowed permits of nine days. By Xinjiang standards he says, this is very generous. I think we better believe him."

A room of uncontrolled waltz somewhere near the desert. There are tonal figurines which continue to collide as a woman sat politely bemused as languages are passed on in the silence of faces. Diplomatic smiles where nobody is talking. Faces which gently contort, sign, disappointed in a minor way. During which there are long pauses. Hesitant moments where the eye can drift and wander. During which an expatriate's attention is caught between the swing out of dresses at the far end of the hall and the call of a window. The long evening's negotiation, after which only the light and the view from a window was release, a light which reminded him of escape from the hypnotism of a school classroom.

After seven o'clock the streets were almost deserted. A time when only the Quranic cry across the river choked by smog could be heard. Part of the evening drone along with desert trains, this call of faith in a city in limbo. By the open window he listened. Arced forward half of his body into the evening air – out of the room of motion to watch the flying silhouettes – those shadows that were going home. Knowing he would rather be out there than inside this room. In the lazy gesture of falling darkness. To be almost in this. Sinking himself into departures of light which signposted the need and the desire to go home. And knowing when to go home to him, as he always knew were habits and traits that only belonged to someone who once herded animals. Cows.

He breathes in the damp air now. All such feelings simply by being near this late light. Then someone is calling him again.

"Kim."

He turns. A voice.

"Are you going?"

In company. In presence. As a child. Whether it was the invited company of western powers or the eastern presence of gods. It was all part of life. The human commotion. As a child he was taught in the belief of this. Raised to understand this commotion. A childhood being full of great company and *presences*. The Mantra. Festival of Holi. Although he himself was never committedly religious yet he would never deny the concept of beliefs. The first time he understood the meaning of presence was among belief, among Shiva. Saigon days in Hindu town before the Viet Cong take-over – a time when he felt such simple things were lacking. A loss. Play. That silent day when the Golden Temple was abandoned, where he heard nothing but flowers and offerings laid before the bolted entrance. Such mourning. And Hindu town was no more. The Hundred Shivas gone away. The times he has carried meat past the sacred temple doors only to be scolded – were no more. Only then did he know the value of existence. Someone. Something. Whether it was East or West.

And a complete opposite was how Ivens, this grand old man of pictures appeared in the desert. His silver thatch of hair like a ghostly creation. In silence, in the barrenness there sat this abstinent *presence*. Camera and reflectives and movements in mirage. How he accidentally encountered all this where there was no life. The figure sat against the half yellow and blue. The almost holy image of this.

In such an irregular place of *presence* he knew one would always feel safe.

Music and dance. Crossing the culture barrier. The Middle Kingdom has always attracted picture makers. Whether memory or celluloid it was that huge plateau once romanced by poets and travellers and great mystics. Over fifty six nations, each of distinct dialectic traditions. Its rituals enigmatic. Its customs defy simple understanding. Yet in spite of all such barriers, a simple dance would be *welcome*. Music would be *friendship*. As did those strange exotic earlier dynasties that still linger, oases and crossroads and cities which have brought together the hearts of all men. And it was during such brief episodes of history where languages first met always the emotional triumph was music and dance.

The closed years after 1949. Outsiders were forbidden. There was the dynastic complexity of access. China closed to the world. Only now and again those names, Cartier Bresson, Michelangelo

Antonioni, Joris Ivens – but always it was nothing more than a rare glimpse. The twentieth century capital of Beijing. During the late seventies things were beginning to alter. There was Paul Horn. There was Jean Michel Jarre. There was communication. By the end of 1980 it was the right time. The availability of the previously 'unavailable'. *"To say Hello through music...."* To stimulate people who *"...were not accustomed to playing with passion nor the variety of colour."* Isaac Stern left such words, such symphonies of hope which ended that decade.

But by 1989 these open years of world friendship were again beginning to alter. The dawn of communication as it seemed was never meant to last.

A lazy desert town. Blue pigeons swerve out from minarets and through into the direct arc of sunlight. From Ikanjubmal they would swerve out the way the pigeons swerved out. Four hundred miles into the desert.

For the oasis Uighur the inner desert was a place to avoid. An abode of curses. The domain of sorcerers. Those that can make a man or an entire city disappear. Legends live long in the sand. In those thousand nights of dust and fire which consume, the caravanserais and cities which were completely interred. Civilisations remained forgotten. Then the early twentieth century saw impressive explorations. Treasures were unearthed. Pagan horses. Graeco Buddhist art. A flourish of cultures dating back even before than that of great wall builders.

He had never been to the desert. Only near, the blowing fringes. So in a way for him it was like an exploration too, an unexpected journey. And who would have guessed but he himself. In an expedition led by the ninety year old film-maker, Joris Ivens.

He said he needed a personal translator, interpreter of the journey. Someone like you. A chance to see desolation six hundred miles long by four hundred and fifty miles wide. Supposedly the cradle of Chinese civilisation. A secret place. Ivens had remarked books and journeys had all ended in the Taklimakan after 1940. Nothing entered. What was the silence of Chinese Central Asia. And Osondaji - the ruins there, that unromanced remainder of history waiting four hundred miles south west of the Tarim Basin, abandoned during the Han era and pillaged seventeen hundred years later by museum collectors – was Ivens' aim. Supposedly a man in search of one's heart.

In the desert track at forty mph. At such an age. What was there to make of such a man? Chasing the wind. Out here among abandoned people? He had in his long and unique career contributed to the world the finest documentaries ever made during the war. In Europe, in Asia. He had known Hemingway. He had known the Revolution, the Hugo and Tramontane. More than fifty years of political film making. But in the desert what was politics and film? What were incidental strangers supposed to make of such a man?

Kim had never heard of him. An old European, he had accidentally stumbled across near the Green Wall at Yulin. *"I want everything to move! And stifle and destroy the desert!"* There was nothing much to make of him then. In the deliriousness of silence. A company of film-makers, their reasons and purpose a great mystery to him. He couldn't have possibly known that one day he would be part of them. Perhaps in a cinema in Toronto or in Paris. Not personally, not in the desert where long ago the cultures of East first met West and whirled themselves till dawn.

A seven day journey through the cool of night. A basic team of twelve. Sound engineers, camera operators, refrigeration units – in two diesel engined vehicles. One fitted with air conditioning because of Ivens' respiratory problem. The translator was always close by. But no one could talk, the engine noise was deafening. If there are roadside cafes – anywhere – they will stop. Near Hadilik they ate tograqh bread, green eggs – which had been buried for three years. They sipped melon tea. During such times nothing passed them except donkey carts and the odd truck out of Kashgar. Rotting canopies surrounded them. Marceline Loridan – Ivens' wife – had been taking still shots. Suddenly she is seen with children around her. They are fascinated. No one had ever seen anything like it. Red. The colour of her hair.

At Andirlangar everyone split up and wandered. One of the vehicles had broken down just five miles out. He had volunteered to stay behind with the driver while the others moved into town for supplies. Two hours of repair under the noonday sun. During that

time there were only tidal waves of mirage. A7909ΦE. The numbers
of a vehicle registration, and a terrible thirst. A drink. The only
thought in him as he now strolled the bazaars. How to ask for a drink
he had no idea. In the northernly dust. And suddenly this hand out of
the shadows, came from within. "You want this..." Then walked
away before he could even thank her, whoever she was. A can of
imitation coke. Trying to remember her name as he pulled off the
ring and tilted the black liquid down into his mouth.

Early Pishan, Axbier, Kalatun, Osondaji, Jingjue, Andier and
early Qiemo stagger westward in a chain of ruins across the southern
end of the Taklimakan. Naked stone remains dating back to the Han
dynasty. Cities which were built directly upon the opulence of
watercourses – which hundreds of years later ran dry. Populations
shifting south with the migration of rivers. And even now ruins such
as Pishan lay forgotten only thirty kilometres from its modern day
descendant. Archaeologists and explorers coming and going in the
name of research. But that was all before 1949. Since then it is said
nothing has changed.

On May 14th they finally arrived at the town of Minfeng, or Niya
as the ancients named it. Two days behind schedule. On the streets
there were red pigeon eggs, a variety of dried fish. Great lance-like
poplars which tower over shackled housing. They stood among them.
Populus euphratica, Kim thought to himself – or *Populus Varifolia.*
Feeling better that there was something he could recognize. From
here he knew Mandarin and China had already died. Somewhere
uncharted - not so deep in the desert were the Tang ruins of Osondaji.
That enigmatic *"Howling Tomb"*. What Ivens came for.

He didn't know she was there. Probably right behind him. He
recognized her right away. Suddenly she moved spiritedly among
them. Pointing at this and that. How the load should be balanced on
camels. How to bargain.

He would later remember, it was something more to do with
timing. With shock and surprise to the natives because of her sharp
demands. In that last desert town. Dexterity. She, who handed him
a drink in such a timely manner. An almost biblical apparition. The
cold fingers which he grasped.

Who was she?

She knew about dust storms. Fohn winds. Knew about the well at Andirlangar built by ghosts in the eighth century. She could read those wonderful Turkic symbols. The armies which rode back and forth almost eight centuries to her, seemed as if only yesterday.

Her name was Ogodai. The expedition would from now on be in her hands. It was her knowledge. This girl who knew the art of handshake, knew how to apply the gracious pressure among strangers. It was her handshake that he could first recall as special. Just that hand. The pressure of it, a soft squeeze. When Ivens first introduced her to the expedition at Lanzhou station. How she bowed and touched the earth with her cold delicate fingers then shook his hands. Stood there in white. Born among mountain snow, she had briefly explained. And no one doubted her. He had not noticed much of her after that. He didn't think much about her anyhow. Not yet.

The biblical manner of her apparition.

"She is a nice girl..." Ivens kept saying from the window of the bus. "A nice girl."

He had said Hallo as he paused behind her. One of the back camels had strayed and was shooting angrily off into the horizon spilling boxes and equipment like leaves falling from an Autumn tree.

"You are from the countryside, are you not?"

Her manners abrupt. Not even facing him. Precise like an arrow.

"I know this." She continued, a brief glance at him. "One can *tell* – my parents taught me this."

"You're not Chinese?"

"No. Mongol."

"Yes. One can *tell*. You're different."

"Different?" And her bangles, he noticed, fell in a sharp sound of brass whenever her forearm is raised to brush back her troughs of hair. *"Different?"* Then running away with that word as if she could play with it. A certain hyperactivity in her character. If not rudeness. At least that was what it seemed to him anyway. The rudeness in her wake which left him staring into the back of her. She had that nauseating knack of catching him in awkwardness, leaving him in awkwardness. Like being told off and left to stand in the playground.

But he told himself he could take it. Another country after all. Different cultures and customs. The displacement of meanings and one's naïve expectations, and in the desert there are such displacements, habit, character, forgetting manners and words and names. A place where there are no names or less names, where you can't remember names. Yes. Perhaps it was because he couldn't remember her name. *Ogodai Dashevig.* From the beginning she was just a figure to him – introduced informally as faces, a part of their company. Someone he only noticed during certain times of the day. She was nothing to him really. In this country you pass through people like gravel in the sand.

But still, what if it was bad manners? So what? Anyway. He felt it was worth it. He really felt more like thanking her. An exchange of responsibility. She was leading them now instead of him. She had taken over *his* responsibilities. No more words. Thinking and then redirecting them. Translation. The headache was on her. Thanks. Here's to you. The pastures now the desert. He was no longer the guardian, the leader of people, the Herd Boy. Instead to be comfortably a part of the nonchalant herd being led by her. And because of this there was something mutual.

Yes. He thought. That was it. A simile.

So in the desert where there are supposedly graceful manners, like manners which offered strangers from nowhere water – he gracefully offered her his position – his leadership and all the importance which came with it. Simply stepping aside. Himself rather preferring to disappear behind camels to become nothing. Invisible to attention.

Cheers anyhow, he waved. Her moving figure in the distance. Nobody would bother him for a while now. The bare landscape marching against him which occupied his daily thoughts. Really no life? No plants? Nothing grows?

At seven-fifteen they come upon a disfigured series of bright yellow walls. Ivens' white strands seems to be everywhere. There was a wailing echo. He turns his head. He does not move. Listening to it. The red sandstone ridge peering over them. *She* is at his side. Marceline joins them both. Nothing else moves. The camel blinking in the wind.

As early as 628 AD Buddhists and Doaist travellers crossing the great beyond have documented *"..strange facts"*. Skimming of ghostly lights. Horses gallop but can never be seen. The legendary Xuanzang noted fires burning among ice, where natives in white robes would dance around and pray. A fire before there was ever sand and wind. But in the desert other than the scarcity of water and the fear of loss, there are desert storms. Documented by all historical journeys. In Taklimakan this happens as frequently as thirty times a year. Those architects who carved towns and desert cities can only leave their brilliance. Obscure ingenuities huddled between orientation and city planning. During the Mongol reign the alchemist Ching or rather his disciple, encountered a *"Howling tomb"* *"..where a number of well placed holes converge down into a cone shaped chamber. As a storm approached, wind is thrust down spirally. Thus explodes air, shifting up dusts and stones – raking up trees and roofs of houses... to such the people will evacuate before time is nigh."*

At night they could hear nothing else but the tomb's *"Warning"*. But Ivens would refer to it as the *"Calling"*. There are small bonfires which start the Uighur guide talking. In the air the smell of roast mutton. He tells them once a long ago explorer had entered its inner sanctum only to reappear back into the light, blinded. Ogodai interprets the tale half huddled along with Marceline and the sizzling fire. Who could tell whether the cameras were rolling or not? Moonlight has replaced wind. They were finally in the region where creatures existed without water. Matters which moved only in darkness. All you could do was look. The ear muted in quietude. As usual he would watch the old man's face against the colour of fire. The flickers on a face, this face of time which anyone can readily find in books and films. A face indexed, archived, accessible. Unlike the wild face which is always next to him. Where would he go to look her up? Where do you start?

Excuses he would dig up when he found himself watching her without consent. But she knew no manners, anyway. How can anything matter? The purge of her lips where nothing is known. A cool face. Perhaps it was the way her face seemed suspended. Her eyes somehow enlarged and growing in the darkness like a cat accustomed to its clarity at night. A quality. There was a quality about her face. What was it? An unblinking quality he could not tell. Millions of faces. Millions of grains of sand. Nothing seemed in place. Perhaps it was the idleness. The shifting desert. A sheet of uncontrolled motion never receding like water. Only invading after dark like the shallow creatures of children's books. Among the ashes of books. What he had heard and read about this country. All customs and manners and decrepitude now planets away. No more of China and her endless exacerbation of people.

He looks into the fire. Turns his attention to the old man. "After the Three Gorges, think I'll go home. Its been more than two years."

At the wisp of dawn he is the first to wake. Clouds like animal fur in the light yonder. Bright gold. Brushing easterly. Rides of dust across the huddle of tents.

He starts shouting into the wind.

"Yol Bolsun." She told him it was how people say goodbye in the desert. Meaning *"May there be a road..."*

"You know. The Chinese are not welcomed here," she said. "There are bitter memories."

"Well. I am sorry."

"Are you Chinese?"

He pauses. "No. Not quite."

"Then why is it you apologise?"

He says nothing.

"Did you know that by tradition girls are *prized* more than boys in the Tarim Basin?"

"Well." He muttered. "Then you are all powerful."

She appeared to smile. Bemused at what he said.

"All powerful...."

Toward the cold evening things start to appear not as they are; shade of dunes look like trees in the distance, the rapid fall of temperature. Two people watching each other through the flames of a crowded fire.

He would always remark on legends and history. The critical authenticity of facts. And she, looking sharp at him, would disagree with him. Placed him into a bracket. *"You are mean..."* Only to ignore him. So that he would know where his opinions stood with her.

As the days wore on the fire was burning less. There was less debris to be discovered. They would sleep earlier to keep warm. The tomb perched high on a nearby ridge, silent. There was no wind nor storm. The crew remained idle. Those aluminium cones which were supposed to catch the voices of wind – record it – were constantly repositioned. He was restless. It was already mid May. It was the interpreter's last night and they all drank Chateneauf du Pape. *"To the coming of the storm!"* Only the women danced. She danced. He watched her again, which was a conscious habit unknown to him in the blue darkness. Her light face picked out by the fire. The music was *How much is that doggy in the window?* There was her whiteness. Her precise glance which, if noticed would disappear again back into the darkness of shoulders and hands. The swinging of their bird-like arms. A Uighur dance he had seen somewhere. Ivens said it was "more like a Pagan dance..." There was clapping. There was absurd music. There was Marceline suggesting 're-enactment' of this desert storm finale. But it was late after all. And Ivens had his reason for coming this far. A chair. A man of great age. The desert. Kim watched. And knew neither of them was listening.

"All through my career there have been no personal motives. This is my first. At my age there is only one regret. I wish one had made more 'Love Stories'."

Such accidents of presence. To encounter someone you would like to be. Some great example. And to Kim, this old film-maker was everything. Was it not for him, he would already be back in Hong Kong.

"Here? This country?"

"You really need someone better than me to answer that question ... Don't you?"

They spoke their farewell at the grey tiled tomb looking like the hump of a half buried whale. He said he couldn't stay anymore. He was *going home.*

"See you in Paris."

Ivens' mane of hair drifting like tentacles. In that devilish whistle. Then turns from him. Assuming as if they will meet again tomorrow – being told by Kim it was something connected with past lives – if you believe such ideas, which was not hard for a man who believes in magic.

"By the way," He turns again to face him. *"Someone else is leaving. Think you better accompany her."*

"She is a nice girl..."

He sat with her at the noodle stall back at Minfeng. The name-plate so long he could hardly pronounce it. She wanted to pay for his. He wouldn't let her.

"You don't know much about this country, do you?"

Rudeness or culture? He would never know what to do about it. Towards the evening there was nothing he could understand.

"Can I tell you a secret?"

"I love what we are doing now. Maybe it was more beautiful before when we were together like a family. For some reason I am most alive at this time of day."

These were the words of Ogodai. They altered at certain times of the day.

It was a silent journey back toward Minfeng.

He had said, "Think a mosquito just bit me."

And, without expression, as usual she ignored him.

"Ah, sorry. What do I know? And I thought no one lived in the desert. No water in the desert..." Half talking to himself knowing she would not answer. Accustomed by now to her unusual character.

But she averts her gaze. And tells him.

"There *were* people and water thousands of years ago..."

To decode rudeness.

She said she was not very alert during the day. That was her excuse. Coming around at night. Born at the winter of night. There was her sombre incarnate at morning. A slow lift toward the evening when she will come around and respond. This was her excuse. *"I don't feel good by day."*

Sleeping faces in a vehicle. Long distances back on that singular desert road. The plan was to catch the express at Dunhuang where, halfway at Lanzhou, he would catch his next connection toward Chongqing while she would carry on east.

It seemed simple enough.

Travelling through the unknown. One knew instinctively how one would enter new regions with caution rather than with communication. What he was taught as a child in Saigon. Warned never to leave the city. Outside was considered a dangerous world. A lawless world.

But who had taught her? The desert?

She said she was going to Beijing. That was all. A language student. A member of the Chinese Language Association. She never spoke much about herself. Only her past. A glorious past harking back eight centuries when her ancestors ruled from China to Russia. "They were known as invaders on horseback." But he would say, "I don't wanna hear it."

She slept mostly during the day. At night she remained wide awake. "What are you? Chinese? But you don't live in China..."

His eye half open. Slouched over the seat.

"You ask me so many questions. Why don't you tell me about yourself for a change? You. Just you." There was a long silence. The darkness seeping warily into him. Nothing but the purr of a diesel engine.

"Why don't you come and find out?" she says.

But he was not listening. Already dreaming.

Her face expressionless. Nothing to read.

"What will you do in Yichang?"

"There's a dam being built there. I know nothing until I get there."

After four days they reach Rioquang. It was market day. Horses filled the streets with dust and people. They came across a stall of mirrors. She was fascinated. He accidentally catches his own reflection. Looks at himself for a while. Thinner. I am changing.

He tells her. "I must get out of this country, soon." They walk through the place where there are rumoured to be *"spirits of the desert."*

"If you leave, when will you be back?"

The vehicle stops at nowhere. It was very late. He was awoken by the jolt. Iridescence of people watching her. He watched her. Pulling her sack behind and stumbling off into the silent vastness. What was going on? He had just woken. Yet he had to pursue her. They were desert companions. And you must say goodbye, which she did not.

"Where are you going?"

She moves very fast. Slipping like a sledge farther and farther into the desert nowhere. He is staggering with his baggage. Bits falling here and there. "Deng-ha! Deng-ha." His cry to halt the impatient vehicle. Faces poised with concentration against two figures running among the landscape. What the hell was she up to anyway? It had gone too far.

You don't know anything about this country, do you?

He caught her by the arm. It was the only way she would respond. Halt.

"Where are you going? You cracked?"

She looked at him through the timid light.

"I want to go walking barefoot in the desert."

"What?"

"Yes. Now."

For a moment he thought there was sweetness in her mood. Both of them motionless. Darkness coming in. The vehicle and the gaze distance away. The horn honking them on. A cry in the sandy vastness.

"Act your age," he mutters.

We were emotional articles bathed of light, he would later tell May, in the presence of a god and leaves and the moisture of another place. There I stood. Enjoying the love of light as if any evening light. Any human being would. But at midnight. And she, mad and abrupt in her movements and manner – pulled me, bit into my skin with her cat-like fingernails – her unexplained guise – perhaps even some unrevealed love. I couldn't tell. Just falling with her down face of that dark dune. Spinning into each others' tumbling arms. Tumbling like hot and cold air. Our bodies in shadow. Colliding in the salt of her forehead. Her fingernails. My foreignness. Two immediate bodies. We lay under this reincarnated light. Who cared how long? Shredding a thousand wings in blue, violet, yellow, then gold. My hand wanting to reach for this light of angels – another hand comes forward and retrieves my outstretched hunger – retracts it coolly and back into the rhythm of a pulsating heart.

It could have been dawn. Could have been anytime after midnight. May, 31st 1989. There was still anger somewhere. Not in me. That smooth face. Was it something she overheard of what I said?

Something critical of Ghengis Khan? They say you can say what you like in the desert. Do what you like. Freedom of expression.

And that Japanese face. A doll. Under this white light. Indirect from it. I could read her face, recognize the Japanese face – the artificial face of a doll which has eluded my memory from the day I first saw her. Broken free of syntax, of incorrect pronunciation. The looseness which spelled the evidence of what I had said. Blunt words against blunt history. The histories she worshipped and adored. Those who were looked up upon as higher beings because they murdered. To her these were matters of pride. Blood roots.

But how was I supposed to know? Know she was listening? Did Ivens know?

Something like a doll. That's all she was to me. In that darkness walking with her I was to discover the *quality* which for so long eluded me. In the linen of white light. The artificial beauty of her face from which I slept. The Japanese puppet-like quality as darkness suddenly fell again.

Still, it was something unusual. Never have I seen two sunsets in a period of one hour. Never.

Being taken somewhere. You follow myth. Enter personal and private spaces. Her excuse was curiosity. She said she had refrained many times from crossing the area. A private zone. Not marked even in scholars' charts. Only a day's walk, she assumed. *Since you know nothing about this country.*

It was in that dried bed of wind. The place traversed from eroded matter to stones in other parts and would unexpectedly revert back to pure sand at the azoic heart.

"White Bone Desert," she called it. "Domain of White Bones." She said it was the one place in Xinjiang's catalogue of deserts she had never crossed. "We must do it at night. No one will see us then."

And he had stupidly asked, "Who?"

She just stares at him. A frown as if to a three year old. She was desert communication. But this explained nothing to him. Had she planned this odd detour with him in mind from the beginning? Dancing with fragrance in her arms. *You are mean...* She was cunning with words, with touch of words. Alchemized senses. It was the way she touched you with words; with feline movements in the frozen darkness. Great silence. Suggestive in human endeavour of emotion. With words.

"Shall we go barefoot into the desert?"

And who could tell where they were? Perhaps she knew. A dark desert. Glittery fragments in the moonlight. He was not used to being awake at night like she was. Two faint shadows hovering across a forbidden landscape. One moving occasionally like a zombie and the other with the singing heart of a child. "Take your shoes off," she said again. "Is that an order?" "Yes." "Is there anything else I should take off since you've cajoled me into the middle of nowhere?" There was no answer. Only that sweet puppet-like face which came only around at midnight. Now seeming to smile.

"You know, I don't have to go to Beijing..." A purring voice in the midnight hour. "...if you don't want me to."

At such time of hour, gone was that stare of challenge. The questioning look which asked of him to prove himself, the look which said; *So you know where you stand with me.* His value in the shade of her umbrella. The eyes as if hate and admiration in one. Unable to leave alone his terrible foreignness.

"If you're like me, since a child, you have been among herds of animals; lived in a *ger* near the sands, you will know the feeling of barefoot. The earth alive underneath you. Knowing what and where you are. Not ever wanting to stay permanent in one single place. Like my ancestors who conquered new lands. I think in the west you call that *"nomadic."*

There was sweetness in her words only at such moments of the hour. A time when she seemed another person. More human. Singing like a harp. Herself. Hope. Desires. It was the only time she spoke honestly to him. Other times she was like stone.

"Are you cracked?" he had bluntly put it. "That is Lop Nur. More than a hundred miles deep. It cannot be crossed. And you *assume* it can be done in a day?"

"There are railways there."

"In a desert?"

"Yes."

"But what for?"

"Want to know something? Yes?" Her moves and words which always held meanings. Putting sand in her pocket at morning, putting his button in her pocket which she yanked off beneath his collar. Rituals and culture. What was it supposed to mean? But he supposed he should follow her and find out.

Which he did.

They came upon clusters of pale buildings the colour of the desert. Surfaces like sunbaked glass sparkling in the moonlight. Walking through the abandonment. Not a word between the both of them. Was it desertification? A city desertified? Embalmed in sand? A vehicle upturned near which appeared as if a force had hurled it like fabric. The ground they walked upon half enamelled. Walls had melted. She wanting to move away – said she felt uneasy. They came to halt upon the ridge of a deep dune. She, still looking oddly haunted.

"And how much more of *that,*" he asks, akimbo behind her as she sat "...is there?"

But she, just gazing up at him. The sad puppy. Remaining like that. No movement around them. There was not a sound. And the sun seeming to come up from behind. Slowly transforming, a confluence of two silhouettes. And he, needing to enjoy the light from the darkness from which she had led him, turned around and stood there. Facing dawn. Eyes closed to feel the warmth. Not knowing the time. And she, unbalancing him with no reason to fall with her together down and back into the darkness that was safety. Away from the light of day. Remaining like that. Wordless.

The only dawn they have ever witnessed which lasted no more than a minute.

Sitting with eyes of steel
he saith, "Don't stand in
my way!" And slipped with a
whoosh! Down hills of phosphor
and lakes of glitter

A puppet quality apparent in her when angered or in defence of self righteousness. No gravity laws governed her movements. What he loved most about her was her guiltless vigour. Something he lacked.

They slept through midday and awoke near dark.

He asked for a translation of her song. The one she would hum but never sing. She obliged. Almost with pride.

"Sixty degrees. North-east. If you're right about the railway this should be where it crosses."

But there was nothing. And she kept walking. Not allowing him to doubt her. Stop her. He goes forward seizing her by the arm wanting reply, an answer. But her body seems to melt at his touch, as if remouldable, without control anymore. A sweetness in her face which refused his gaze. Her eyes at the sand. In his presence, in his touch and in his gaze she became a limp almost lifeless puppet. Not a word between either of them. He is never sure what to do when she is like this. What was happening? What had been happening? A small fraction of her body so malleable in his hand. What was it?

For another few yards she kept silence. Afraid of him. Until he stumbles and falls. She is coming to aid his foreignness. Kneeling down to him. "I am alright," he said. Then the cold metal emerging from what he had kicked.

A rail buried under sand.

"What did you do that for?" Her eyes intense again.

He had just lobbed away her shoes and his.

"If we don't hurry and catch the train, by noon our 'soles' *will be burning in the desert.* How would you like that?"

"You are not Chinese. You are crazy."

"And you're not?"

They were going to jump the train. There were no stops in the desert. No such policy. That's if there are trains. They followed the half interred iron track now and again half holding hands. So to prevent either of them stumbling. Half conscious of each other as responsible adults. Only realising they were almost lost. The face of a compass and then her error-free face. The excuses because of the desert. The profound solitude. It creates questions with no reply. Both of them the same age.

"You're very good with history. Why don't you tell me what happened last night?"

"Last night?" she replied, hardly taking her eyes off the track.

"Yes."

"God knows."

"But you know. It was no holy light. Because you knew what it was. Why not tell me another secret?"

"I think it is almost dawn...."

She's dodging the issue again, he thought. Should I hold her and shake it out of her? Shake out those silly meanings? But he was wrong. She seems to be listening hard in the thin cold air.

"Do you hear it?"

He quickly knelt down. His ears against the cool rail.

But he could hear nothing. "It's the wind."

But she would not move. Her attention glued at the evolving yonder. The dim distance. And for a while there was nothing. Still two figures strolling the beach with no water. She giving him that cool look again.

"I am certain you are no Chinaman. You know nothing."

"I agree. Nobody is ever themselves in the desert. I know that much."

"Do you? Truly? Even in zones of twentieth century death?"

They were in the accompaniment of acoustic dunes when she mentioned the word "test".

"Harbin. 1945. The retreating Japanese army let loose laboratory rats carrying the virus Hataan. It killed millions. Did you know that? 41.5° north, 88.5° east. They explode bombs in the desert. With great care and great secrecy. So in time the desert is the rubbish tip of eternity."

"You think I love the desert – don't you? I understand her terrible fate. People hate her yet she is beautiful. She is mystery. No man ever knowing enough about her to feel safe, yet she has always tempted them, lured them to cross her poisoned belly with discoveries of rich cities and lost treasures. Why did *you* follow me?

"Why?"

And for some reason her voice mattered no more. He was not listening. In a sphere of viscosity because he had seen the train in the dull horizon. Coming closer to be misinterpreted by wind. The ticket out. And then neither of them could say anything, could not utter a surprise – as the miraculous express exploded from nowhere. Suddenly the desert silence shattered.

He could remember telling her to aim between the carriages – to run faster – keep watching the speed of the train and not her naked feet. He was telling her not to let go no matter what happened.

Simply barefooted. Ignore the pain. The differences in the desert that had come between them. So slow and then so fast. No time to react. And sometime later they were to be drinking sparkling wine. Facing each other in locomotive privacy like two stone lions at a palace gate. The desert sealed away between a window. Among faces. Unsure why they were laughing as the alcohol brewed away his terrible foreignness and her brooding rudeness. They had come out of Lop Nur. They were moving fast like dreams written in books. Moments precious. Things from now on would seem very fast for them. They were heading far east. The year was 1989.

It was because, he thought. Because. Barefooted. It was not anything else. Barefooted. The way this touched his heart, bringing up childhood in a swirl of Autumn leaves. As if she knew of him – what most a person privately treasured. *You are a village boy, are you not?*

At Lanzhou he stepped clumsily off the train. Anxi, Jiayuguan, Zhangye, Shandan – landscape so swift. To be back at Lanzhou, the city of smog. Not certain why he was glad to be out of the desert. Not sure why she didn't wave to him from the moving train. His head held high, arced at heaven yet aimed at her. She probably will always remember him this way. Poised at her for letting him go. Not letting herself go. The steam and evening smog soon drowning out everything. Nothing but the whistles warning. The bench of drunkenness. Bottles. Alone. Pulling down the cloth screen against the unwanted faces that hover. I will visit Beijing one day, he had uttered. I will look you up. Goodbye. And she could say nothing. Smiled awfully which she knew he could detect. Then hating him more for saying goodbye again

Perhaps it does matter where you are. It was the way she said nothing. Sometimes saying everything. The way she said it. A memory which can stroke the bareness of a human heart.

So at the right moment, at the right time. He stepped back on the train. Her moment. Evening.

"Don't you have any bloody manners at all?"

She looked up with surprise. With hatred in her eyes. Then flings herself onto him. Her chin over his left shoulder. A white screen falling over excess motion.

The train bustling dutifully east.

What was happening? In a few days he would be in Hong Kong. In a matter of destiny they will be together. That was the plan. And plans can change.

They had forgotten. They had forgotten they were both in a continent of tumultuous change.

CANDLE FLIES

AH-FUNN, OR THE MUTE GIRL as she was better known, glides
within a labyrinth of dust. Greeted always by the cries of hunger.
This old man. These wild unwanted creatures. Searchers of the
night. Sometimes her clutch of hair swinging like Wagtail.
Sometimes free-falling over her face like madness. She moves
capriciously but does not dance. Only the quizzical flop of her
sandals. As she edged closer and closer with the evening shade under
porticoes and armpits of stone, always carrying her basket she would
suddenly be half greeted by a whirlpool of three colours. Rinsing,
sniffing the perimeter of the shrine and the old man. Their wet noses
poking his leg, white and grey twisting at the lower roots of his body.
Calling. Touching him in endless gestures of worship.
    She goes forward now. Touching him. He is still real. But the
expressions of worship had already scattered as if a fallen meteorite.
Leaving debris of cautioned eyes hugging near corners and shrubs.
Reticently sculptured. A family of spies. She cannot touch them.
Not feel them like the way LoudCracker feels them. His morphologic
language. How he can breach the shrill of silence like the crow of
dawn. His voice of rifles. She touched him again. Food. Affection.
The arrival of swift darkness. He staggers up. Groaned. And began
emptying the scrap she has brought into the bang of alloy and then into
the music of a ceramic dish. Banging the pot again until it is hollow.
Where she may enjoy watching them eat at close range. Imagine what
it would be like to stroke under their furry chins. Head to tail. Fear
to love.
    They will know you one day, he tells her with a squeaky giggle.
A habit she loved. There was so many things she loved. Unwanted
things. Discarded life. This very much being her world. The tap at
the mango she most loved. Washing her feet. The open welcome of
the forest and the uncle god. The cats which oscillate her old man.

He warns her about the one eyed cat, or Pirate as she named it, who always sat around them like a bag of assorted fluff. Not to be fooled by her absence of fear, the cool stance, the black dot still looking more like an island – which even dogs fear. Unstirred but drifting. Sometimes motionless. But she does not heed his warning. She admired her calm. There was no doubt out of the entire gang whom she loved most. This crippled unchallenged leader. Seeming not in the least afraid of people nor the wander of dogs as if her lack of vision displaced the prediction of fear. Or simply as if she had seen much and was a kind of professional at all this. LoudCracker had assumed she must be the mother. Mother of nine (seven now). He said it was the crooked tail, the black tail. None of the other cats had this feature, only her. But whichever way, the mute girl favoured her most because of her unwavering stance. How she sculpted herself as others scattered with her approaching body. Afraid even of the hand that fed them. Only the hollow socket of an eye. The one eye pleased to see her benefactor. In the eye of darkness where many things are said but nothing is seen.

In the rapid drone toward evening solitude. The machines over the clutch of valleys weakening, dying off across the border. Fading into echo where vehicles are heard rambling in the distance.

Kim had arrived later than usual. Four miles before the village a gnarled figure appeared by the roadside – waving for help. Following her he came to a hidden cluster of houses – mostly lifeless. Under old trees he entered with her into that great familiar architectural darkness. The mirror inside forever facing the doorway as prescribed. She leads him toward that strange object smothered in shadow.

He picks up the phone – speaking from one district to another.

"They will fix that road lamp in two days," he tells her.

She asked him to stay for food. She asked for his name. She speaks like a child.

"Must you go?"

Because no one in the New Territories ever wants to be left alone.

All evening we gazed at the old murals. Our heads arced like stargazers. We argued about the ideograms, the shapes and resemblances. Kim said it looked more like a langur.

I say it looked more like an old lady squatting over some spring onions.

The day before he took me over the south valley. Where they were due to build a rubbish dump. On the way was the part of the river which was deepest. As a child he was warned of its 'bottomless' trait. We bathed for the last time further up where water is born – or was. The bulldozers move in tomorrow. It was our last dip. I felt very special there. The silver birches and kingfisher which accompanied us.

PS Litsea glutinosa B.B. Rob. (Pond Spice.) A rare tree, he says which here seems to have developed a love for water among other things. Ephemeral tranquillity.

During a night of rain LoudCracker would awake to discover water scorpions. In the ubiquitous puddles twaddled among raw earth which were once foundations of a house. At noon the Mute scrutinising them. Once thinking them ugly and useless, now, thanks to her mentor, she refrains from stepping over them. *No. They are good. Get rid of mosquitoes and insects.*

There is the sand wasp on which the old man has kept watch since his arrival. Every now and then in a different area hauling upward into the rotten eaves with its huge catch where it has formed a cocoon.

See that? Where it stores the live prey. Lays the eggs. And there the pupae can grow and eat at the same time.

But she yanks her head from left to right in total disagreement. Refusing to believe him. Preferring that old house wives' tale about the mysterious *'Sting of Metamorphosis'*.

LoudCracker always simply giggling. And he continues to admire the prey the wasp captures, which sometimes appear to be larger and larger. The cicadas that change colour and habitat and die with the change in seasons. Enamelled life. Click beetles. Feathers. An old snake skin. The moth pupae like the shape of a thumb which swung east, south, west and north at the touch of sunlight. The table within the Ancestral Hall full of such sacred debris added day by day. Intruded by wild cats. Holy relics according to a world of play.

It can't be helped, he kept saying. Things must move on...

Relics special to a wild mind. Kim bringing her a cube from the desert. "Loess," he tells her. Releasing a fine magical dust when rubbed in the hand. His curious gifts which she loved, which capture the wild mind. Things which are worthless. But difficult to obtain like a pebble deep in the river. It was rare for him to visit before May came. Now he could arrive early as afternoon. Noodles, melons, luncheon meat and news. What he brings from a destiny somewhere in the city distance. They all are pleased to see him with a desire personal in their hearts.

25th April. At Peng Che

I have never seen Ah-Funn happier. We were at the birthday of A-ma Neung. Our equivalent of a local goddess. She is celebrated annually. Through wars and invasion. Her temple being as beautiful as Christmas lights. Thronged in a procession of people and dragons and tigrets and seamonsters and garlands of prayer where the three of us had to hold hands so as not to be separated. There was traditional theatre for the old. Its songs and dialects amusing to us. The mysterious 'Pao' which each team of celestial monsters fought over. In earlier times this often resulted in bloodshed. Kim thinks this prized object may be a section of a holy mirror.

The old man must know. Maybe I'll ask him tomorrow.

The Gun Tower ascended five storeys. Kim had broken the lock and was leading her up toward the darkness. It was past noon. There were no windows. The shutters all closed. They moved up the zig zag of rotted stairs hearing the groan of dried timber, termite-ridden. The walls falling with geckos. She was hesitant but cool. Sometimes exploring in front of him. An old chair or the hooks on the high ceiling. She was determined that these things should not frighten her. "Have you been here before?" she asks him, forever aware of one's trespass. He opens the shutters which were wedged closed by bricks. The light aerosol entering. The room suddenly transformed. A light of comfort.

"No light. No presence. How long has it been like this? This room?"

Stroking the backs of dust-coated balustrades he touched her shoulder. "Wait here." The last staircase was more narrow, defiled. "Careful!" she cried, as the wood broke away under him. The room suddenly seemed to be crumbling. "Kim?" Then all she could hear was the terrifying squeak of the last bolt being turned. Feel the rust of black iron, the friction. The echo silence filled by this sound now which seemed so frightening. If not rudely awakening.

"Kim?" She could see nothing. Then the squeak stops. Then there was excess light. Blinding her. And his hand reaching into darkness against heaven saying, "This way..." And then when she was halfway up the stairs and every thing fell under her – mortar and plank smashing below her – her legs in mid air. Feeling the hold of one dusty step and then that tensile arm and that grip which was accustomed to gripping her in mid air on a swing, since childhood.

He hauled her from the vault darkness.

The Gun Tower silence.

They were no longer surrounded by anything. Not trees nor hills nor darkness. They seemed to be above it all now. Almost touching the sky.

"Alright?"

"Yes."

"Are you sure?"

"It's OK." Her breathing still uneasy as she said this.

"I should have known about those stairs. But it's been such a long time. And even *I* forget."

But she is already exploring again. Swiftly moving from his standing body. A hunger which he recognizes.

"These slots – are they for arrows or guns?"

"I am not sure." He wanders over to her. The area no bigger than the smallest bedroom. There was a miniature pavilion. Half colonial fashion, half theatrical.

"I suppose the rocks *are* for pelting bandits?" Her voice lightly mocking. Leaning against a pillar.

"Perhaps. Don't think they got very far though. It was less communal defence. More about the power of the man who owned it. His life and times which still testifies him. The kind of power which enable him to feel he owned everything. Destiny, people, villages and cities..."

And then she had said, "I didn't love him, you know."

And he, without a word, his hands over the low roof of the pavilion, knew precisely what he had not wanted her to say ever since the moment he rebuilt the swing. Not wanting to realise she had a past after their childhood together, not caring about that missing paragraph as if nothing had happened between the years they were lost to one another. Destiny is destiny. Now that was all that really mattered to him.

"He was the kind of man like this building. He could offer everything. He inspired my ambition.

"But I never loved him."

"It matters not to me."

"No? But I want to tell you anyway."

"Why?"

She drifts from the pillar. Peering into the city distance.

"When I was sixteen he took me to a Picasso exhibition in London. It was my birthday. And I love art. Originally I intended to study art. I wrote about Picasso in my thesis and had my room full of his nudes. I thought cubism was really trendy."

A quarry explosion shattering the air. She is temporarily distracted.

"Yes. I really enjoyed that evening. Relishing the atmosphere in the Tate. You need to understand Picasso's early life in order to understand his work and his style. I knew so much about him. Don't you think if you are to love a person you need to know about them first? True to the heart, I mean. My heart."

"I sound silly don't I?"

He turns his head. "You make perfect sense."

"I only wanted to be loved. You know it's only human. I showed that man what I loved. I thought it was very true. I showed him what I loved and he in turn showed me that he could never love what I deeply love. And from that moment I knew he would never understand me. Not the true *me.*"

"But why run from him now?"

"Who said I was running?"

Kim smiling to this answer. Knowing her hardness. Then replied: "But I am." And she was smiling to his reply.

"The entire population of this colony is running. Except you, May. Because you're smarter than them. You're almost English. Your ticket with Wordsworth and Scott. I can't remember who said 'Students are great cannon fodder in the hands of clever men.' I suspect that's probably quite true."

"That must have been a politician," utters May.

"No. A Hong Kong newspaper."

"And you believe that?"

"Yes."

"You surprise me."

"Remember June 4th 1989?"

"Oh, you mean the massacre..."

" ... what a surprise, eh?"

Another explosion now. This time the suddenness startles her. "It must have been terrible. All those students gunned down cold-bloodedly. I was so angry."

"Were you? Why?"

"Those were my people – that's why." she says. "Don't you have any sense of nationality, Kim? Don't forget you're Chinese as well!"

"Yes." His eyes in the light. As if unconcerned. "But what's it for? What good will it do? So you can fall back on it when the present fails to work?"

"Yes." She was already distant from him as she said this, perturbed by his remarks. The pavilion shadowed between them.

Cranes smoothing south westerly. She, giving him that prosecuting look. "And why not? That's my country."

"A place you know nothing about? The world knows nothing about... A faith and a nation your parents fled from? Where they saw no hope? *Is* that realistic?"

"*Yes*. I don't see any problems with that."

"No? Well. What do I know? A country is like a person. It can love and reject you. I've always wondered how this can make sense. You just said a moment ago the requirement of the heart was to *know*. And now you're telling me different. So where's the education in this? The true search of the heart?"

"That's different..."

"Is that right?"

"Oh, leave me alone – I am not in the *mood*!"

She swings out her back against him, irritated. Not wanting to argue anymore. Then she starts for the broken stairway.

"May. Don't leave. Ignore what I said. Can't help talking like a grown up, sometimes." And such words caused the girl of the swing to stand still. Suddenly to realize they were immobilized five storeys up. Both remaining unmoved. The occasional churn of peregrines which signal a storm.

"Let's just talk about the Sacred Swing..." Till the mute girl walked by looking up for the first time to smile and wave at the architectural monstrosity which has scared her since her days of education.

"I loved smelling the Yellow Orchid in you," he said. And walked away into the echo of barking which floated near darkness. The road pushing out to a curve near the foliage of banana leaves which forever seem to dance coquettishly in the breeze. He looks back at her once. She waited till he has reached the bridge then called out to him.

"*White* Orchids!" And saw him pause to her words. "White Jade Orchids! Michelia alba DC!" Then he waved. Acknowledged and understood, and corrected. Waving once again and to finally wave goodbye before his tall figure vanishes like a trick. Sometimes the mute girl chasing this disappearance act on her BMX. Along the mauve road.

And May would go and pack up the soap and towel by the tap he had used, then light the mosquito repellent. Darkness advanced in a matter of twenty minutes. Between the sinking of the sun and the chorus of night insects. At such moments of solitude she wrote best. So tense before her friend is due. The surprise. A movement that is never predictable which slipped as fast as night. Bringing back the news that Kim was on his last ride out. Tempting her long lost desire for the city.

Punti are natives. Meaning 'My land' or 'Local'. Hakka are guests. Meaning 'Invited family' or just 'Guest'. Our adopted uncle tells me in the past there were bloody territory wars because of land. All over south China like tribal wars. All because of the difference in language. Dialects. In 1950 there were more than 4000 Hakka veterans of the Long March. Most of them high ranking officials. Revolutionary heroes. Yet their backgrounds were kept secret fearing the concept of dialect may once again provoke another break up of the Chinese kingdom. Womenfolk in Hakka are traditionally industrious by nature. Self reliant. It is still an incredible sight for me to see them labouring on roads and construction grounds. Those Polo Mint-like piths like my Aunt used to wear against the heat. Of course when 'Guests' migrate into cities or into other worlds they too eventually will intermix and become natives or 'Locals'.

I am re-learning all these things which Kim thinks will matter little. He is more concerned about his 'trees'. For him, looking up at the leaves is an almost holy act. There are three old companions by the swing of our youth. Cerbera. Chinese Banyan. The Camphor. He picks up each leaf whispering their names like long lost lovers.

A national rubbish tip is being excavated just over the next valley. I think he fears for them. The old companions, I mean. His childhood. Our past.

Trees are very important, I agree. They predetermine how the future of a place will look. The health of the land. How suited to habitat or industrial amenity. He says it's important to have trees which give shade and use to the people in places of harsh climates. Recorrecting the environmental mistakes. He spent a number of years in China doing nothing else. The most prominent tree anywhere here is the Longan. Fruits in June. It is Ah-Funn's favourite tree because you can discover special insects there. The sap attracts them. Her personal passion is the Candle Fly. An ugly insect, I think. It has a peculiar elongated head like a trunk. A tongue or proboscis which it inserts into the bark. But it does fly bright. A fluttery yellow. You could call it the Longan Fly, really. Because it lives nowhere else.

'Fulgara Candelaina. L.' Exclusive only to this part of the world.

He would post her letter by air mail each time he headed out.

Who is this friend of yours? Kim had asked. You keep writing but she never seems to reply...

Never you mind, she says.

No more flip flops. May was late. She heard the vehicle coming near far away. Ah-Funn who stood at the doorway in a white blouse and navy skirt was in her best tonight. Her dark hair combed down in a pony tail, red ribbonned. Hoydenish but less wild. With proper shoes which sparkled. Still nagging at May like a wagging pup. It was all the bath's fault, she kept explaining. The water taking so long to boil. Unlike her friend who bathed under a warm shower of the courtyard tap, May simply could not oblige. Running with the dress now, with the clatter of heels again. The flower necklace in place which she had earlier collected from the tree of White Jade Orchid. Almost feeling herself like the bright blue streak of a kingfisher. Through the forest and through the school gate. The paper lanterns dangling above her. Lifting up her skirt as she ran.

She entered the awaiting classroom. Lit entirely by candles placed on top of inverted desk legs which were coordinated to appear like pillars. There were paper lanterns too. The mute girl seated by the old man among corridors evolved of school furniture. Both of the apparent guests turning as she approached from behind. Passing them. The old man letting a gasp. May's dressed figure in the lantern glow. Her fingers brushing the dust, the bottles of Asti Martini. And by the panoramic blackboard stood Kim. The host. Beside the only paraffin stove. In his shorts. Straw hat and chop stick-looking raggedy. The sizzling sound of frying which filled the darkness.

The Host? She starts to giggle at him.

"They say," he says, *"'only in your dreams'*. I know it's only in your childhood." He goes forward taking her hand which is covering her laughter, taking her delicately by the fingers as if for a dance. She spinning for him. The flames picking out the happiness in her face

"This *is* for you, Kim. This *is* the Laura Ashley for so long you have requested."

Then they glided in silence. In the manners of a school classroom. Supposedly a school reunion intended for Master Wong. Who would soon be with them. A man whom they all loved. Who taught them English, taught them about the Weeping Willow. How during days of festivity it warded off evil. A man they remember who loathed anything Japanese. And in the cramped streets Kim had met him where he told him about May. The only girl who had a dress. A peculiar manner who left for England.

"That is the greatest of jewellery. The greatest perfume! What a surprise when Master Wong sees you, or rather picks up the scent of you. The three of us – as we were. What a surprise."

"Is his wife coming?"

"You remember her?"

"Why shouldn't I? She was the one who administered sweets during tears. The lady of cuts and bruises."

"Yes. Wasn't she?"

They danced together moving past the tables, unsettling each candle flame-throwing motion into shadows and flicker. Till the classroom seemed alive in the presence of flight.

"You dance beautifully."

"I had lessons. What my mother insisted a decent girl should know."

"Travesty of dance near the desert. I learnt it there."

The rim of her dress skating across the flames. Kim's grip tightening when she moves too close. Her hair sometimes too close – whipping across his face like blades as if no longer aware. Her steps now confident. No longer aware of disturbance. Not caring as adults in this introductive dance. Laughing and applauding.

"Very good!" cried LoudCracker as he and the Mute cheerfully clapped away. Not aware of their disturbance, the whole room, the forest, the uncle god, inhabited by their private reunion.

"You two should get it together..."

And May, blushing – pushes herself from their format of dance to wander over to the burning stove. Browsing here and there.

"What's the banquet?"

"You will like it." And the Herd Boy returns briefly to his preparation. Throwing in prawns which amplify the sizzle. Exploding the flames – the entire classroom clearly lit over many seconds. Exciting the mute girl while LoudCracker simply sat there. Haunted.

"Squid and vinegar. Scallops and ginger." Kim calling out each dish. May and her friend arranging the desks to form tonight's dining area. They waited as long as they could till the steam left the food. They ate as much as they could. Held up their mugs of tea and glasses of wine. They would soon forget the reason of reunion.

"Did I ever tell you two about Autumn Worms? I think I told Ah-Funn." LoudCracker mostly sipping tea now. Making his pardon about a small appetite at his age. "In summer they are caterpillars. Then in winter they are weeds. They are harvested and used as an aphrodisiac."

True or false. The night is all around them. Some half believing, some not sure, and there are some whose world is entirely based upon nothing else.

Night noises and celebration. A time before a place and its people are to be returned. Handed over. A reunion. A coastal fragment long desired by what LoudCracker calls the Tang Frontier. Four figures gathering near the approach of a possible guest. Some are dressed as they were in school uniform. A blue dress. A Herd Boy. It was about childhood and nothing more. Things lost and found. The mute girl and her possession of cats. May with her letters of curiosity. Kim washing at the courtyard tap. And this old man nearing the end. None of them permanent in this derelict village, this forsaken place of long memories. Each there for their own reason. For memories.

"Here, Ah-Funn. A compass. This will work better than moth pupae." The Mute girl jubilantly accepts. Showing it right away to her special uncle. While Kim turns to face May.

"And this is for you." And takes her by the wrist.

Undoes her watch. Then replaces it with his. "Rado. 1967. From my father's business in Saigon. It's never left me for anything."

May could only smile.

"You're mad. I can't accept this. It's too valuable to you."

"That's why it's a gift to you."

"But why tonight? What's so special?"

"For memory. I must remember tonight. All of us must remember tonight. In case we never meet again."

"Don't say that."

He was about to speak again but she moves up, silencing him. Her left hand cupped against his mouth. While always in the silence was the chuckle, an old man's giggle.

"He is right, amoy. He is a smart boy. And you will not find many like him."

"Yes. You're right, uncle. He is odd..."

"How is it that you two are not yet married? In England? In America? You should go as soon as possible. No good to keep coming back here. There is nothing left here for you. Not for anyone. You two need to be modern. Go far away. Look far away. Don't look in the darkness. What is there? In darkness there is only the past.

"No words can express how grateful I am to you all. Ah-Funn here, who loves nature. You will go one day and I hope you may never return. I will soon be gone. Dead, I mean."

"May Tai Wong protect you three."

They were all looking at him. For a moment silence reigned. The mute girl nodding to the old man. Heartbroken at his words. His sweet chuckly words. This reunion. Celebration. It seemed, as midnight walked in, all this was ending through words.

"Don't talk nonsense, uncle."

But LoudCracker was not listening, not responding.

"At my age there are so many things to be scared of. At my age death must come. Only the escorts of death. *Life is transient. Death is pre-destined.* They say he wore silly ochre jerkins. The worst of humour too. But I think he may be something else.

"Never have I been scared of the unknown. Never Red Guards and never the dark. Truly. I am half Australian, half Hakka. We have always gone where we desire.

"Now, I will go where *I* desire."

There was still no sign of any visitor. If there was silence between them now, there was nothing but chirping overtures. The voice of night.

It was almost 4 am when May awoke into the hollow darkness. No night cries. Absolute silence. The candles had all burned out. She edged herself up. Careful as ever, which was her character. She got off the table from beside Ah-Funn, they both sharing the same blanket. Slipping back into her stilettos. And left her there among all the debris of food and bottles.

There was no sign of the two men anywhere. But since LoudCracker was rumoured never to sleep she had assumed obviously he must be taking a stroll. Perhaps Kim had joined him. A father and son relationship, she mused. She began smoothing her way through the desks recalling what they had done only a few hours before. The four of them moving to Ave Maria. And suddenly there where other lesser movements at the window or half entering among them, noticeably not human but nevertheless still guests. Cats accustomed to leftovers. Ah-Funn amused by their surprise presence. Somehow all of them together tonight as if at a graduation ceremony. So glad. She kept saying to him how glad she was to be here. To be with him as now.

Once out in the playground the echo of her footsteps was suddenly amplified. One's own intrusion surprised her. Like the stillness of portraiture. Not even the haunted bamboo moved. Two of the paper lanterns were flickering. Almost sleeping. Nothing awoke except him and her. The time now being so blue and she appearing to him in a blue dress like the night before, like the child many years before.

He moves over to her enshrining her with his own bodily blanket as if he had been expecting her, as if it was his turn to await. Welcomes her into his morning curfew.

"I am getting my old job back, May."

His chin brushing her forehead as she sighed.

"Did you hear me?"

She sighs again. Now hugging him. He was smelling her hair like the way he would smell flowers.

"In Central District. It means I can't come here anymore. Do you know what this means?"

But she remained wordless. Agile. Then he realised he was holding up the entire weight of her body. Her head rolling to one side with her hair like water falling. It was not yet dawn. Not the time for words.

The comfort of sleep in the arms of someone you love.

The other day they caught some birds. A Bulbul. Pair of Red Munias. Then yesterday they caught a poor porcupine. Kim was not impressed. Our new uncle had so much time on his hands he could find nothing better to do than to build cages. Ah-Funn seemed impressed. But Kim scolded them both. I think the old boy would probably have eaten the porcupine was it not for Kim. He set the pig free but allowed them to keep the birds.

But this morning – somehow – both the Munias disappeared. The cages empty. Except for some feathery remains. Kim concludes it must be the work of hungry night serpents. Out of remorse he sets free the Bulbul. Saying "If only I had let them go last night!"

I told him it was not his fault. There was nothing he could have done. I don't think he liked what I said. I suspect a Herd Boy will forever be a Herd Boy. Forever feel responsible for every little aspect of life.

This much I can understand about him.

You are a strong man. You bathe in the springs of winter. Springs which I am honoured to prescribe are good for the spirit.

He then checks the pulse at the smuggler's wrist.

But I fear the excessive dreams will continue. But here, before you go, see this Fungi – Lingchih. Saprophytic on roots or dead Oaks. Before sleep. It will keep them away. Keep the dream of gods away.

It was a fascinating face, he had thought to himself. Primate moves. A living apothecary.

But who really *is* this man?

Then he woke. LoudCracker awoke.

Realised he was no longer in the jungle. The Ancestral Hall and a flurry of cats enshrouding him. It had been his first long sleep. About an hour. It was still dark.

Who was this man anyway? He had thought even in a dream. He could never forget. Who was this man who could tell at the feel of a light pulse – a person's life force. Propinquity of death or the nourishment of fruits. Read a vein or a look of a face like numerical charts.

The weapons had lay as a graveyard of decay in front of them. All around *them*. The sentry of Langurs. Cries smothering this awesome dump of metallic capability.

Where do they get them from?

Who sells such things?

Hua Tuo looked at him. His eyes prosecuting – kept them on the Tang man until he spoke.

I don't know.

"A physician. A pioneer of medicine. Discovered the acupoint method of *jiaji* during the Three Kingdoms Period.

"He lived one thousand and seven hundred years ago...."

May is half giggling.

Kim puts down the book. *Legends and Myths of The Middle Kingdom.*

"It's not that funny," he says. Drying himself while she sits mocking during what appears to be another humid Hong Kong evening. Then he turns to her, increases the throttle of the tap. And with the thrill of fresh mineral water turns her irritable giggling into laughing screams.

OUTRIDE

KIM AND MAY ARE HAND IN HAND wandering through the forest of intermittent childhood. Daylight applied through cirrocumulus filters. Among familiar bird songs. Near water again. What she loved most. Touching and walking into familiar things. Themselves. Watching themselves in the reflection against the heaven's whiteness. The watery distortion which at times almost merged them. To dissolve them as one. Only a kiss away like two swinging bodies blended together by light. In a deserted village. Supposedly uninhabited.

"I remember the fragrance of blue."

They watch each other in the rippling mirror. Not blinking. His eyes leaning from behind. Always a set of hands that seem to guide her. Wrapping her like she wrapped Ah-Funn.

"Who are you now?" she finally asked in her playful mood. A finger at the lip. "I knew you once. Air washing my ears. On a swing. When you were half naked like Sabu The Elephant Boy. Except you kept cows. They called you the Herd Boy. You played alone. That silly straw hat. But where are you now? Are you still among those whispery pastures? Sleeping?"

"And you," he added, staring her out. "Still the Blue angel?"

She jerked her shoulders - pushing him back slightly as if they were upon a plank dangling on air. A childish fall. "Stop looking at me! I *hate* it when people stare."

They headed back following the stone path which LoudCracker swept almost every day except when there was rain or a storm. His blood prints undetectable now. As if the old man had finally been successful in wiping away the evidence of his own trespass. It must have been nearing June. Another rebirth of cicadas. There was a quivering breeze when Kim pointed up at the trees as they approached the second deity which guarded water. Like a baby throne of mortar.

Cups and wax candles and joss sticks – all the dedicated work of Ah-Funn, perhaps acting mostly under the advice of LoudCracker. And May would occasionally join them. Adding her advice on what she could remember – which was not much. Kim then returning to find with surprise a ceremony entirely re-invented. So even as the village was truly deserted it somehow kept in an illusion of life by an odd number of simple chores.

"I love the name David," she said. "They are always so human and honest. But if you ask me in reference to women I would be lost. I simply don't know who is best.

"I suppose we, us two are fortunate enough in being christened by names which work well both East and West. *Yours,* I think could do with being a little more precise. More informative. It does sound too much like a short cut – if somebody didn't know you well."

And Kim, doing nothing more than a glance. Agreeing unconditionally. Most of the time just letting her talk. Her voice which now as it seemed filling the last remnance of his childspace.

"You know, May. When leaves die they die in beauty. It's the most beautiful stage you'll ever see in its life. Something of a graceful end. I would wish that all life, including humans can go in the same way. End like that."

"*What?*"

He turns to her. They halt near the Sacred Swing. Near songs. "Can I tell you something?"

"Why?"

"Because..."

"...You love me."

"No." He replied, stroking both his hands through her cool hair. Looking down directly into her eyes. The woods suddenly silenced around them as if it could listen. "But I believe you should at least *know* what I know. What little I know. Miss Picasso."

Somnolent light. Shooting and fading through the leaves and flowers. He picks off the white Pavetta from its illuminence and hands it to her. There is no longer the sound of water now.

"You two kept shouting for me to hurry. I was talking to him. Remember? That day when we were due off to see the festivities at Peng Che. Although you two probably didn't see it, we were reading a journal. Completely Chinese. I could hardly read some of the words myself because of the Pinyin problem. But I knew he would know.

"Anyhow. It was an interesting chat. But mostly he kept arguing about the dates. Figures and numbers which are not always apparent to a normal reader. He said the excavation dates were wrong. For instance he said the Terracotta Warriors were unearthed much earlier. 1935. 1938. According to him."

"Sounds like he knows his stuff." May half muttering to herself. Still sniffing the flowers.

"The journal was called *Kaoguxuebao*. Published by the Chinese Academy of Social Sciences. In other words The Institute of Archaeology."

"Meaning?"

"The Institute of Archaeology was set up during the 1950s by a Professor Xia Nai. It was the only institution never to have suffered politically during the period of great purges. During the Cultural Revolution. What you might call a night train which never stops. It has been responsible for some of the most important archaeological finds in the world. History being big in China, you see. Every step you take there is history. Dynastic remains, precious swords, burials. There is enough excavation work in that country which will last well into the next century. It's one busy institute. Scarcely anyone knew of its existence nor activity until 1973, when cultural departments in Beijing and London agreed on a first major exhibition at the Royal Academy."

"How do you know all this?"

"Hang on. Let me finish.

"The Institute of Archaeology is government funded. Meaning Government owned. What I know is this. Its activities are highly confidential. So also, are the people who it employs. And, sometimes they have been known to explore the earth not always in the likeliest of places.

"So you see my point? Maybe once long ago he was a very important man. Once upon a time.

"This is a very uneducated guess by the way."

May sat on the swing with her spectacles. The thin pages flicking through her fingers, the black and white photos of faces grouped together looking so blurred, all now seeming to her the more she

looked as if they could be someone. *Him,* perhaps. Uncle.
LoudCracker.

"So. You knew all," she said. "All this time you knew more than
Ah-Funn."

"I was part of the Lanzhou Institute, remember? I was there on
and off for two years. But as I said all this is just one fantastic guess.
There's no real evidence."

But she was undeterred.

"But he could be working for the Beijing Government. The names
responsible for ordering the massacre of 1989..."

"Maybe. He might have even sold arms to warring countries.
Sold death just for profit. But the point is he was once a very
important man. And now look at what he *is,* what is left. He *must* be
the castrater of cats."

"It's not funny. They are murderers. He could be a murderer."

"We don't know that."

"Yes we do. He has dark secrets. There's something not right.
You know that. Why are you defending him anyway? Why have you
been hiding him?" She rips off her glasses. "I don't understand *you.*
Why?"

"Well. I am an ordinary individual. I am standing up for the
common cause and common rights of a common man."

"Common man? Him? Ah-Funn does not know better. But you,
Kim... I think you're just blindly defending him!" She leaps from the
air and marched from the forest.

"Where are you going?"

"What do you think?"

He takes her by the arm.

"Don't do it, May! You don't know what you're doing."

They stare at each other through the splintered light. Their
opinions divided.

"This is Ah-Funn's law," he kept saying. "This is her only world.
We can't interfere. We mustn't. If we broke in now, we will be no
better nor less ignorant than any past colonial government. No better
than any reclaiming government."

"Let me go!"

"It's Ah-Funn's law, May. Remember that! If you love her. She
was the one who found him. Not us. She bandaged him, fed him and

has taken care of him. We are outsiders to all this, to this village. This culture. We must not interfere!"

But she runs from him. The wind in her ears now. The branches and shadows warped. She is out of the forest. I must be mad! He must be mad! Both of them. This village insanity. Harbouring a stranger. She walks across the dusty road free of twigs and loose gravel thinking about nothing else. Time to go. Yes. Leave. There is nothing here. But all she could hear as she approached the tap by the mango was sobbing. Uncontrolled wailing. Ah-Funn walking sombrely towards her. In her arms slung the lifeless body of a cat.

"Blasted dogs!" growled LoudCracker who was hovering from behind. "A dog. I know it. Been here many times. This one was not careful..."

May gently intercepts her. Not looking at the loud voice. Wiping away the girl's tears. Just kneeling there with her. Silent.

"Nay worry, amoy. We will have more kittens for you soon. Soon."

While May stood in the shadows. The girl soon drifting from her. She lets her go. There was nothing she could do. And she knew. A distant explosion as she stood up. If now she were to turn around she knew Kim would be there. The journal rolled up in his right hand like a statue of law. Ah-Funn's law. He was right. The echo of dirge drifting through the village.

Nothing more of opinions now. Just two people remaining simply staring at one another.

She sees this boy of mud and herd. He stands before her. He is going to join her on air. Two children. But now they are kissing.

NEAR TAN AN MEN SQUARE 1989

Two people. They had come out of the desert. A city evolving around them. Sometimes one is walking faster than the other. As if in attempt of losing the other.

Ogodai, he kept saying. Are you alright?

Near seven p.m. she was seemingly awkward again, like a stranger. But loving. Affectionate in her stare. He had never noticed this before – only on that night of the mysterious light. Like a pup who misses her master. Bright eyes. A river of clarity. Lifting up his right hand against her face – within her lips, concealing coded kisses in his hand like a letter.

They had arrived in Beijing when sand fell showering from a desert 150 miles away. All over the city. The monotone commotion. Cyclists. Trucks. Straight boulevards. Kim stood among them disturbed by the noise and dust. So distressed to have come out of the solitude and suddenly be dropped into all this. While she remained relatively unbothered, as if the desert had followed her.

They emerged from Xizhimen Station at about three p.m. and headed south through the city. She was wordless again. So cool. The net scarf whiteness around her face. The wind in it. I am looking for someone, she said. She knew where she was going alright.

The city during this hour is tense.

They moved into the square. Into the unbelievability of presence. A gathering in thousands. Banners and slogans.

What is happening? He asked her as they cut diagonally across the millennia of faces.

A demonstration, she replied. Democracy!

And threw her arms around him. Hugging him. Then he realised every one else around them was hugging too. Embracing for the need of it.

It must be the city, he thought. People are affected by it like an allergy to dust. A fear of excess, of crowds and alien noises. They act awkward for a while.

I don't like it here, he tells her.

He had awoken. And there was an aerosol of light. An apple. A window. There was a girl half naked. Her wing-like shoulders sometimes in this light. In the moving train there was an apple sliced in half.

The same love? But somehow they were out of the sparseness. Out of the desert. And she suddenly seemed hungry. Hungry. Starved of wishes. Every moment a metaphor of touch, a glare or the cold way she swerved from his gaze. How she held him so tight in the madness of traffic. In the beckoning crowd. Her palm like sap squeezed of juice. Transforming. Gripping him. The students around them gripping each other. Comfort. As if a farewell.

To disappear into the tumult of history. Emotionally vanish. I wonder if she ever knew that? Into destiny.

During duller days in the village the old man would leave piles of dead leaves burning. The white smoke withering for hours. Even by dusk there are sparks carried up by wind.

They watched the smoke nearing darkness. She tells him she was part of the demonstration in London after the Tan An Men Square incident of June the fourth 1989.

He tells her I was actually there.

My work was to bring life where there was no life. To protect life against other more powerful forms of predatory life. An amnesty of nature, I suppose.

But in the desert there was no life. The barrenness which filled the spirit. I was nothing in the desert. My skills as if powerless. And there, among the Bauchan dunes she was everything. Like a well. Every step you took she was consulted. We did nothing without her. She was a vessel. A destiny. Flickering pages in the sand. I never thought about it till now. But I did envy how she threw about her presence. A plasmic power. A lady of light. White lady. Almost like the one erected in the Square blowing of blood red sand in 1989.

There were supposed to be three things which did not blink. The sun, a snake, a hypnotist. In the Great Beyond she did not blink. Bright eyed. Less oriental in the darkness. Which one of these was she? The inner comfort when she stared. Such sorcery. Which one exactly? He had followed her into the starless desert. He had followed her into this crowd. Was it simply seduction?

There were two explosions in the thickness of air. The oceanic crowd shuffling. And that was how he lost her. In darkness, in panic.

The time must have been near ten p.m.

He kept shouting her name. Only a moment ago he held her. How did he lose her? This damn crowd.

In Heaven's Gate Square they were separated, an area where if you erased all ancient relics and modern statues, all memories of lies, was this grand ocean of skies. Where the horizon ends in the distance of a red wall. Burning. Nothing but fire and ocean. This pure imitation of heaven. Where if a person eased back far enough into its darkness and nothingness he or she could disappear like a pebble leaving not a trace.

Ceased to exist.

She was leading him. She was holding him, or was it he holding her? But it was different this time. There was no more solitude and the desert. There was this damn city crowd.

He did not like it.

Dashevig? No answer. What was happening? Through this mass ephemeral geography of faces he was calling her name. Ogodai? His hands darting in air. Ogodai! Suddenly there was no time to say goodbye. There was nothing he could do.

The bodies that were falling in the darkness. Soldiers, civilians, students. How many bodies were collapsing around him he could not tell. The effect was diverse. Mostly fires in the distance. Martial law. Silhouettes which ominously split before the blazing machines. Machines and screams which clash.

A fiery ocean.

He kept running. Dodging when he saw a flash or a burn. Not sure what to do in the flare of skeletal remains. How long had he searched through the wreckage of humans? Faith? Democracy? Freedom? When did such bloody things matter? How to die for what you believe. In the carnage, in the loss – this blasted crowd which she had embraced and hugged with trust which had swallowed her like part of himself. This can happen when you've been together in the desert. If only she had listened. Let's leave, Ogodai. I don't think it's safe. Who was that man she was introducing him to? Excess of faces. Falsity of emotions, impatience, this last tango. He could see she was in the whirlwind. Riding it high at night. Her desire for modernity, for the West. And all he wanted then was one person. Her. To take her away from all this mess, words, ideology, a new regime. He had seen it all before. Such things had destroyed his childhood. The wonderful culture commotion. People. But it was all too late. It was destiny.

Her cat-like fingernails which suddenly slipped from his grip. Slipping like satin.

And everything was burning.

She was leading him. She's gone. No. Can't be! Her swift stridence. But she is gone, even *her*. This power. Which he felt he himself had never had – and wanted. What would he do now?

The fires burning around him. The screams. He finds himself closing a huge door which sealed off the blasts and firing. He doesn't know where he is, where he had run. A room somewhere off the street, a temporary hiding away from the bullets. Thinking. She's gone. He doesn't know the time, what to do anymore. A lost herd. A lost leader. This place he knew nothing about which she led him to. But she's gone. And now he waits. As if for death to enter.

In the muffled darkness. Feeling soaked. Sweat or blood he could not see. For a while remaining there. Just the noise of his own exhausted breathing which seems to echo in the unknown darkness. In shock, against a wall, below high windows. His fingers brushing along the black wall. The cold surface which he felt against his fingers. Touching marble. Everything so cold. So dark. The eaves and switches. He flicks one of them on.

A circle of light deep in a void of darkness.

Then as he looked up, he sees that he is among more artillery, tanks again. The turrets pointed at him. Great silhouettes stoned before this appearance of light. The cannons that hang around him within the exploded ceiling. The fascist pillars which emerge. Then, in the stillness, he suddenly realises he is in a museum. Beijing Military Museum of Revolution.

He enters among the old war exhibits. Half running when he hears more gun fire from the street. Pacing himself toward the spotlight at the far end of the hall. All the shadows which envelop him as he progresses simply in the need to progress because there is light. Still unsure what is happening. All down to impulse now. Reaction.

He enters an arena of illumination. Objects in cases and in glass sarcophagi in their symmetric display of glare. He passes all these war relics, like some deep blue sea. The artificial lamp above him is high. Invisible. As he arrives closer to the source he moves more slowly. Suddenly not caring about time. In the rifles, the photos, the flags, the straw sandals worn in 1935, while outside the vehicles were still burning. What was he looking for he didn't know. Just there that's all. Coincidental. Reincarnated souls. Hiding. Grief. Alone. Just ineptly browsing in a war museum.

Joris Ivens. A great friend of the Chinese Revolution.
The Camera of 1938

Accidents of ambiguity. Such encounters. It was crucified against the wall. He didn't know how long he had been reading the ant-sized letters. A box. Mewed high in the void above him. At first he thought it was some first aid kit – *break the glass for fire axe.* But moving closer he realised the display was much more important, it was canonized. The height was beyond normal human reach. An object with a handle. Weapon-like. Till he read the words. *"The Camera of Revolution."* And recognized the name. Joris Ivens. While gunfire is sounding all around him. The door which suddenly smashed open and in poured soldiers. The street of fire finally entering.

Living without you. Swans and cranes and egrets exploding in a dark lake. Her. The way she led him. Living without this. Suddenly to have lost her. He was alone. But one is never alone, never wants to be alone. He breathes in the air, the exterior which he loves. He had been alone. He finds himself running for his life. Running with the object in his grasp. So in the darkness he had been alone. Plunging sheets of dust. Lost among the fire of humans. Then out of the fire – a camera – a name. He had been infinitely lost until he found such reasons.
A name. An inspiration.
Something that mattered in the chaos. So during such hours of desperation it was important to know you were not alone, feel not alone. Such accidents of ambiguity. In the desert or a museum.

Such encounters in desolate places. Perhaps someday he will find out what it all meant, someday.

But now he is running, seeming never to stop. Across a small sea and away from the fires of pursuit. Across oceans. Not ever looking back, not knowing what pursues him. Pushing his way toward the forest of Soong Ching Ling Children's Science Park. His mind on another journey, a rendezvous. Nothing else matters now except to make his way into the future. Out of this city. In the swaying of branches, the cries which emit among them. Creature chants. The cicadas, the monkeys, the thousand arrays of wildlife which he has suddenly disturbed.

And the hush of night...

He had smashed the box which held the camera, broken through several back doors. He had climbed walls. He had come across through an empty bridge. But no matter how far he ran it was not far enough. Those fires in his mind – her destiny – what really *did* happen to her? She said she believed in sacrifices, in purges, in past grandeur. Things he saw as madness. Without reason. Without goodbye. Without you. And all for what? Dying for a cause. Dying for a crowd. Did she really think it wrong to simply be alive? To breathe, love and remember. Well? Through the dangers of frantic history. What's wrong with the desire to stay alive? Like Ivens. Ninety years. And now as he breathed in the air of creatures – their crackling movements which he has entered upon – the sheltering wood's darkness, he felt such reasons. Their mass of reasons.

Whether he fell out of sheer exhaustion or tripped on something, he didn't know. He fell. The 1926 *Bell and Howell 015 FK* rolls across the earth. A silent fall. The night calls dampened as he laid there.

When he gets up he is in a City Zoo. Plumages and lawn. A boy. There are no sounds. There are cages around him. Animals. He is in the centre of them all. A jungle crossroad. Paw paws and palms and willows strung up and falling down over dark cages. He stands so still by the disused fountain. Nothing seems to move unless he moves. And if he moved, say nudging left, he will see the reticence of one clouded leopard, or a little to the right would be the similar posture of a snow leopard. While behind him are the birds of paradise. But that's only if he moved. And he does not. He stands perfectly still by a cart of rotten meat. He has fed the animals from what was left in the stores. A zoo starved of almost three days. Out of nowhere a boy came and fed them in a time when humans feared the streets. As if human time had stopped altogether.

But he is still because he is watching the black panther. Love and fear. Suddenly a whistle is near. But he is not yet eleven. Not just anywhere. The animal silence abruptly shattered. The cages falling apart. Animals loose. Wings of freedom. Knights of the jungle. What explosions were like in 1975.

In the roar of traffic. Buses, trucks, taxis. He remembers invisibly entering them. The street lit buildings and shimmering dust of night Beijing. He keeps pushing through it all. Reflexes, reaction, memories, somehow that was what got him onto a tour bus. A late cruise out of the city. Somehow he was intercepted. His Cantonese, his Hakka, his foreignness was passport during that moment. The vehicle heading westward. There was no panic nor guns nor tanks. He had entered normality again, another world.

While somewhere the fires were still burning. Whether reality or dream. The crowd or the desert. Somewhere a reincarnated light. United them. Burnt them. She was in his arms. What happened? A sacred light, he had thought. A message in the darkness of a desert.

The vehicle continues to drift westward.

She leads me in like paper about to burn. Among the Singing Sands, which was once a sea – once the waves of "*innumerable laughter*". She had come with me through the silence. The crowds. You understand?

We were emotional articles bathed in light.

HOW TO CEASE BLEEDING

*If you're ever somewhere and wounded – if there is no immediate help
– no one around to help; no civilisation.
This is what uncle says you must do*

*The procedure henceforth is to write these words on a cloth, any cloth,
then bandage it round and round the wounded area.
He says this was the ancient art in the cure for bleeding.*

By the time he entered the unremembered village road there was already monsoonal rain and thunder. Wind swinging menacingly into violent twists and dances and into banana leaves. Darkness and shimmers. By the time he reached the small bridge there was a massive flood. The river had risen over the bridge. Only its black rails were visible, which he used to cross, where there normally had been a fifteen foot drop into water. If there was lightning he could see the outline of the Gun Tower, if not there would be the beacon of the patrol post located north of the hills. The velocity of rain advancing over him. There had been non-stop rain for three days. But tonight there was a storm. And he had not been back since. Now hurrying in the rain. His shirt and jacket soaked through. He had not heard from her at all. She had not phoned him. He was worried.

There was debris of branches and twigs as he proceeded. The road which is normally spotless was now obliterated of its cleanliness. In the belch of light he was cautious of the beckoning Gun Tower. Nudged and bullied, its old body crying.

He called her name, banging on the huge doors. When she opened up she flung herself onto his wet body. Lightning greeted this unison at the doorway. Then blew out all the candles.

"He's gone!"

"What?"

She kept shaking her head.

"I can't find him..."

He took the torch from her and made a splash across the rippling courtyard. She followed him. In the wind and the collapse of shattering shadows. Slates smashing down before them. She was in her flip flops. The rain was warm. Every step, every possible moment in the fort objects were falling from the night, twigs tumbling – large and small. When they touched at the doorstep of the Ancestral Hall there was not a soul. A flask, a blanket, a bowl. No man. All there was of whatever it was. In the noises in the roof being torn by wind they searched, Kim half knowing he would find nothing, but he had to make sure. Then a *crash!* from the roof at the far end. A great branch stabbed through. Pieces flew. Bringing raw wind and rain and perhaps, one day from now, sunlight.

In the forest there was no rain. They knew it was the last place to look. In the waltz of Camphor and Cerbera and Fig leaves. Where the old man was supposedly found. Here and there the wild thrash of movement. The beam of a torch light. Two figures.

"Uncle!"

They kept calling in the wind and thunder. But there was no reply. Nothing. The only trace of presence was of a god and a school and the great lingering of trees. The orchestration of branches in the crackle of bamboo. Two people forever searching, it seemed. Their past, their togetherness. Perhaps a destiny. Perhaps someday such encounters will mean something. A swing. A girl. As if in a dream.

Then he takes her by the arm. Wet fabric against white flesh. Takes her fingers as he looks up into the oceanic branches. Leading her back out of the forest and away from the Sacred Swing moving ghostly in the wind. He takes that look of a girl which spelt I will never leave you. Her conserved silence he loved.

Still, the shattering cries emitted among the echo of trees. He only looks back once.

Near wind. The old man had waited in the forest. Sometime before or sometime after it was difficult to say. Things happen as they are. Dreams. Swinging above him through the sound of shimmering strings. The absolute silence. He knew it was time, the hiatus of cries, the sudden manners – he knew it was ready. Like the night before.

Now he must go with the Langurs. In the light beyond the forest and a god. Soon to be somewhere else, soon to meet *him* again. And as he headed into this light only one question remained conscious in his head. How did you manage to live so long?

The creatures marching up behind him. The evolving light warped in the trees. Stars soon dissolve behind him.

> Sitting with eyes of steel
> he saith: "Don't stand in
> my way!" And slipped with a
> whoosh! Down hills of phosphor
> and lakes of glitter.

> Sitting with eyes of steel

And sitting you will still see,
"Don't stand in my way!"
And saith a thousand times more
And the "whoosh!" that shall follow.

Darkness. An opening. So slow. The doors groan out of decay.
Kim's figure emerges from the light. Somewhere there is an old
bicycle.

In the first sign of sunlight the village appeared in shipwreck.
Fragments of walls and tiles and branches littered everywhere. Much
of the fort had crumbled away in the storm. May's courtyard was a
sea of debris.

Three figures moving towards evening. Only the accompaniment
of laughing doves. They had gathered and salvaged what they could.
In the damp dark interior which was the residence, May looks back
for the last time. She sees the reflection of two people in the mirror.
And for a moment it seems to her one was unsure of who was who,
which was which. She slings the sack over herself. She pauses.
Then together with Ah-Funn they pull at the doors and finally push the
lock into place.

Kim is already waiting under the ruined Gun Tower. Still staring
at it, still studying it. Only half of its previous mass is standing. As
if a blunt sword had come down on it diagonally. He stands by the
stick frame of a bicycle against the rapid disappearance of light. The
two approach him over bricks and mortar and the fallen tree. They
are like sisters. They are like shadows of each other.

"Go home, Ah-Funn," she tells her. "Don't stay here, OK."

They hug. Kim watches them and smiles. Then kicks the wheels
off its stand and gets on. Soon May steps on with him. She sits
behind him with her face resting against his back. He lets the bike
roll free down the small hill. They move shakily away from the
stationed figure. She waves goodbye to them. She does not seem to
alter, does not move.

The village hangs in silence. Nothing moves. Sometime from
now the hills which surround the village will burn. Midnight
incandescences. No one will know how it started or how or who it
was lit by. The hills will be charred. Rare shrubs be erased and new
life shall begin. Very few people will be around to witness this except
her, this girl of silence. Anyhow, perhaps she has seen it all before.
Nothing is of great surprise to her. She knows things must change
like the metamorphosis of a pupa. She understands what it is to be

wild, unwanted. And as the big tom cat plunges its head favourably against her naked left knee, twisting around her repeatedly, she knows also this was affection. Understood it was jealous of a rival tabby she had been stroking. The sea of three colours which now lovingly encompass her. The Ancestral Hall refurbished by life and branches and, when there is dawn, sunlight.

The road ahead of them darkening. They are riding away towards the light of the city. He feels the rust on the handle bars, the presence of her arms worn around his waist. They both feel the cool breeze, can hear at the same time that soft never-ending squeak down by the unoiled rear wheel. They soon pass inhabited settlements. Figures that are still working near dark. In the high barricades, the watch posts, the flame throwers among the agricultural fields.

As they rode away into the distance the knight-like road lamps began to flicker. Then replace the colour of the disappeared sun.

Acknowledgements

Though some of the characters and happenings are based around historical data it is important to point out that this story is fictional, and so are some of the places and situations described.

Many great books were very important to me during my wanderings, and I would like to list some. *Desertification: Natural Background and Human Mismanagement* by Monique Maingeut, Springer Verlag 1991. The poem on p 88 is by Du Fu, *The Heights* in W.J.B. Fletcher's translation from *The Bad Earth* by Vaclav Smil, Zed Press 1984. Quotes I used in "Reincarnated Lights" p 120 from *China Builds the Bomb* by John Wilson Lewis and Xue Litai, Stanford University Press 1988. Also in italics p 166 from *Chinese Central Asia* by Sir Clarmont Percival Skrine, Oxford University Press 1986.

I quoted (in italics) Isaac Stern's words on p114 from *From Moa to Mozart* of the 1979 China concert tour (*1980 Hopewell Foundation Inc.*). While on p 115 there are also words of Joris Ivens from his last and most mythical work *A Tale of the Wind* (*1988 Capi-Films*). The *Bell & Howell* camera which Kim repossesses on p 163 was the original equipment actually used by Ivens in 1938 which he "left" for the Communist guerrillas near Yanan. May's diary entry on p 62 is *Clerodendrum fortunatum L.* (Fire Hand-lit by Ghost).

In particular I must thank Professor Roderick Whitfield of the Percival David Foundation of Chinese Art, for his kind and sincere attention which parented my curiosities. Also the Natural History Centre at Liverpool Museum and Roger Haige. There were the seashore memoirs of Mrs Fu Kiu Lam-Cheung, and the nomadism of Julie and Judy. My thanks to Gina Leung, Bill and Pat Pudney, Sheena and Pat Harlin, Andrew Waddington, Kuldeep Hoonjan, and the Ol' Man, I didn't let you down! And especially my Aunt and Mother for their Histories. Big brother was the "Herd Boy". Finally to Tracy and Peggy: TO TELL YOU the secret love affair was really this book. For Jo and *his* world.

"Good Hunting!"

To the memory of Locusts, then. The Grasshoppers. Sudden surprises. The *catch!* To the fires, then. The flames we follow with a bush and with an eye for a frying *catch!* To the plastic bags with holes – to the handy wicker cans with esoteric rubber lids with which you held your *catch!* To the memory of those you met immediately after school. The Gang. The Dogs. Those hills. To the man who came late on bicycle. The Buyer. Stockbroker of the thousands *catch!* Bursting sounds within those panniers with which he buys your *catch!* "Alive" To your *prize!*

    Bravo! then. To the ones that get away. *Bravo!* To the Gecko lizard who leaves you its *tail!*

    And to those who took you there. The days that took you there. *Thanks!*